FLY

Casualty Sister Dawn Campion is strangely reluctant to volunteer her help for the newly-formed Isle of Wight air-ambulance service. After this inauspicious start to her working relationship with the dynamic Dr Miles Stratton, how can she possibly survive the proximity inevitable in such vital work?

Books you will enjoy
in our Doctor – Nurse series

FLYAWAY SISTER

by

LISA COOPER

MILLS & BOON LIMITED
London · Sydney · Toronto

First published in Great Britain 1983
by Mills & Boon Limited, 15–16 Brook's Mews,
London W1A 1DR

ISBN 0 263 74232 6

Set in 11 on 12½ Linotron Times
03/0383

Photoset by Rowland Phototypesetting Ltd
Bury St Edmunds, Suffolk
Made and printed in Great Britain by
Richard Clay (The Chaucer Press) Ltd
Bungay, Suffolk

CHAPTER ONE

'I WISH I was back here,' said Dawn Campion, to the casualty sister of the Princess Beatrice Hospital in South East London. 'Are you sure you have time to have a cup of coffee with me? I feel guilty coming here and interrupting you when everything looks so hectic.'

'It's all right. I've finished for half an hour,' said Sister Isobel Horner. 'I'm glad to see you. I wish you were back with us, too. Any chance of your leg being better in time to relieve summer holidays?' They went into the small office that was not only office, but consultation room about all matters concerning the nursing staff in the department, Sister's rest room, if she could escape the notice of any passing surgeon who smelled her coffee brewing, and the place where notes were lost and found with monotonous regularity as surgeons, house surgeons and casualty officers flitted through it on their way to and from cases.

'I came up to see the Prof,' Dawn said. 'He said I must be on light duties for a while. As my contract here was up the casualty department in a small cottage hospital seemed ideal as a place where I could work and yet not be over-tired, have an interest and breathe some fresh air.' Dawn smiled. 'That part of it is heavenly. I love the Isle of Wight . . . I lived there for a while before and still have a few connections there, but everyone I knew has moved on or got married and I find I have little in common with most of them any more.'

'Is the work so very boring?' Sister Horner sighed. 'What I'd give to be slack just for one day . . . It must be quite an experience to be bored.'

'Stop teasing me, Bella. You know that you hate inactivity as much as I do.' Dawn moved restlessly and sipped her coffee. 'I can't put my finger on it, but there's something lacking. While I was here, training at dear old Beatties, there was always someone to be with for offduty, plenty of social life and the work was fascinating. Would you believe that the only case I had one day was a woman with a bad splinter in her hand? Nothing more . . . it was hardly worth getting the department untidy for that.'

'You could have more patients if a certain scheme comes into being,' said Isobel.

'Don't tell me you're evacuating the Princess Beatrice to the Island? I know the old girl's namesake lived there when Victoria was on the throne, but that's carrying things too far.'

'I'm serious. One of our men—at least, not a Beatties-trained man, but he worked here for six months before he took his fellowship and became a registrar—has moved South and wants to set up a voluntary air-ambulance service. It would be based on one of the big towns like Portsmouth or Southampton, but would liaise with coast guards and accident units all along the South.'

'I don't see how that could affect me.'

'It might well do. The sea around that little island can get very rough and there are the added dangers of the double tides and the broken tide races round the headlands off the Needles, aren't there? I've been there for a holiday, but even when the sun shines, the sea has a sinister swell beneath the West Wight.'

'Local ambulance services deal with all that. They know what to expect when boy scouts climb cliffs and get cut off by the tide and they cope beautifully. The local life-boat service is superb, too, with a long history of fast efficient help mostly on a voluntary basis. I can't see another service fitting in at all,' Dawn said, with a frown.

'Look out for him, in any case.' Isobel smiled. She hesitated. 'You aren't still thinking about Arnold Guester, are you?'

'If you mean am I still in love with him, the answer is no. In fact, I doubt if what I felt for Arnold was love . . . not the real lasting love that would survive the kind of trauma that we went through.' Dawn smiled sadly. 'It certainly didn't last with him, did it? or he would never have panicked and run from the car when it turned over, leaving me hanging by my safety straps.'

'The safety straps saved your life, love.'

'But if they had been cut as soon as it happened, I wouldn't have had a triple fracture of tibia and fibula with all the accompanying complications.' Her face was pale. 'I never want to see Arnold again.'

'Well, the last I heard was that he had taken that job in the States and left last week. He's a good administrator, if you can give him his due, and I think he'll find a niche for himself over there.' She laughed. 'What is the talent like? Lots of robust and lusty fishermen and bronzed sailors? Fun and games at the sailing clubs and knees up at the Young Conservatives?'

'One or two are all right for a drink after duty or a pub lunch. There's a man from Australia who surfs, even in this weather, and he's rather sweet,' Dawn said, but when she tried to visualise any of the men she met during her day at work or in the small village close to the hospital, she found them blurred as strangers are blurred when she had no lasting interest in them.

'Then you just have to meet . . .'

'Don't tell me. I don't want to know his name. Haven't you learned yet that to say that two of your friends will like each other on sight is death to any thought of mutual rapport? If I meet him and like him . . . fine. If I meet him and loathe him and he hates me, then you will not be embarrassed, and I shall have only myself to blame.'

'I can't see any man hating you, Dawn.' Isobel laughed as Dawn stretched up to take her coat from the hook and fastened the buttons of her blouson jacket over her shapely hips. 'A pity you have to wear trousers all the time. What do you wear on duty?'

'I wear a slightly long dress which covers the scars if I have thick stockings and it doesn't really matter who sees my limp. I have nobody to impress.' She glanced at the clock. 'Oh! Is that the time? I shall have to fly. I can't leave it late getting back as the last ferry is mid-evening at this time of the year, before the holiday rush begins.' She sighed. 'It isn't far, as the crow flies, but when I have to cross London to Victoria, catch the train and then the ferry, it's a cold, tiring journey.' Her heart-shaped face was pale under the thick auburn hair and the troubled green eyes were 'put in with smutty fingers'. Isobel smiled as she recalled that saying, almost forgotten from her own country childhood, but so apt for the lovely girl who had trained with her and endured the miseries and triumphs of life in a major teaching hospital.

'Take care,' said Isobel. 'And don't forget.

If you get a chance to meet Dr X. don't snub him because you think that all men are brutes. He's very good at his job and might need a little light relief before going into the Air Force in November.'

'I don't feel like being light relief for stray, idle males, thank you. I want to get fit and able to come back here. Keep the job warm and I'll apply for it formally as soon as I get back.' She looked round the austere office with affection. 'This room is quite, quite hideous, and I love it. There are memories that started here . . . and happenings that I can't even believe, although I was here when they happened. Do you remember the night they brought in that street fight?'

'I thought you had a train to catch? You could stay overnight . . . I can arrange a bed for you.'

'No, I have to go. I have an appointment with physiotherapy in the morning and they've been so good I hate to mess up their appointments.' Dawn picked up her small suitcase and holdall, walking fast but still with a slight limp after her accident. 'Goodbye, and it's good to see you again, Bella. Don't forget that I have a spare bed if you fancy a weekend walking and breathing pure air. Why not come for Easter, the week after next?'

'Are you going, or aren't you? I'll let you know. I'd like to see where you live.'

Dawn went out into the pale spring sunshine.

Tired plants that had struggled through the winter were trying to shake off the smog and cold and raise new shoots. A few brave daffodils brightened the grey walls of the old hospital and from a bedroom window of the nurses' home came the sound of laughter. That's what I miss, she thought. I haven't shared a silly joke with a gaggle of nurses and students for ages. She shrugged her holdall higher on her shoulder. Must be getting past it, or just not meeting anyone with my zany sense of humour.

She found a taxi fairly easily, which gave her spirits a lift. She slipped into a corner seat on the train and decided that life wasn't so bad and settled down to read a magazine while the rails hummed the message that she was going home. Dawn stared out of the window. It was strange how one part of her life was so completely left behind as soon as wheels started to turn, taking her to the other half of her existence. Beatties, her friends and her past were all drifting further and further away. The fresh fields were green and young and the trees had that air of expectancy and youth that April brings to England in the South. She swallowed hard. It was beautiful. It was as beautiful as she remembered it when she travelled between her parents' home and relatives on the island where she spent school holidays. Flooded fields told of spring rains and the water in the twisting streams was silvery clear. Surely, this upsurge of yearning must die? It couldn't happen every spring when the sap rose in the trees and the birds mated? She tried to focus her thoughts on friends . . . on places she would visit when she could walk again with her customary ease. This sensation of being on the brink of something must fade . . . it was the cruelty of Nature making the world ready for new life . . . and love, when her heart was empty and she had built up a hard casing behind which she intended to shelter, never again to be vulnerable to the charms of a chauvinistic, charming and completely unreliable man. Her eyes filled with tears of self-pity and she rummaged for a tissue and pretended to blow her nose as the scent of damp earth and sweet tiny leaves came to her through the open window of the compartment when the train slowed at a junction.

The rush from train to ferry took all her attention and concentration. Although her leg was no longer painful, she was almost afraid of steps and slippery slopes in case she lost her balance and fell again, as she had done during the time when her leg was in plaster. But, as usual, the passengers jostled each other to get on the ferry only to find that there were more than enough seats waiting both in the saloon and on deck. The men waiting for the cars to drive on to the vessel, up the ramp and into the dark maw of the boat, stood laconically watching the foot passengers hurry up the narrow gangway. One man called a greeting to a passenger and heads turned to see who he was addressing.

Dawn smiled. It was beginning already. If someone called to another person on the tube station in London, who would bother to look, or even recall it happening? But here, it was quite interesting, as if the man recognised must be known to the whole boatload. Of course, most of the passengers were locals, either from Lymington or Yarmouth, commuters or families returning from visits. In a week or so, the queues would be longer and the faces those of strangers on holiday for Easter. She settled her luggage by her side in a window seat in the main saloon and watched the sea birds skimming the bay under the bright sunlight. It was stuffy, and too good to miss outside, so Dawn gathered up her bags again and tried the deck. There were several people sitting on the seats over the life rafts. Most of them wore thick winter clothes as if they distrusted the golden gleam of April and the false cool brightness of the sun.

The seat under her cotton jeans was hard and cold and she shifted about, hoping to become warmer. It was still better to be in the fresh air than in the smoky saloon, so she buttoned her jacket high under her chin and pulled on a pale yellow knitted hat that hid most of her hair and made her look even paler and more like a lonely little waif. She put her rain-coat over her knees and felt better. She took a deep breath. Tomorrow, I'll walk and exercise and do everything I can to get fit, she vowed. A sea-gull screamed at the whistle that blew from the funnel announcing that the ferry was about to start, and the engines churned.

Two men wearing dark woollen jerseys and knitted hats talked while leaning against the side of the boat. She recognised one as a man who had come into casualty at the St Boniface Hospital for advice about a rash that had appeared on one arm. He stared at her and half smiled, wondering if the pretty girl who worked in the outpatients department could be this rather frozen female in the yellow cap. He turned away when there was no answering glimmer in Sister Campion's eyes. That's all I need, she thought. A nice discussion about Bert Cass's skin! She looked out over the sea and watched the small sailing boats hanging on the fringes of the white wake of the ferry, ready to turn into wind as soon as it was safe to do so. I'd like to sail again, she thought, and her pulse quickened. It would be exciting and she might meet one or two people of her own age, with her interests, or at least have someone with whom to spend offduty in the warmer days to come.

A man stood by the life-boat davit. He was tall and yet well built. His dark thick hair flew out in an untamed mass, and, in profile, the cleft in his chin gave him an air of power and strength that was compelling. An empty space around him added to the illusion that this was a man alone. He should be standing in the prow of an invading ship, thought Dawn. He should wear a dark red cloak of rich velvet with bronze buckles to secure it on the shoulders while he urged his oarsmen on to greater efforts. She shook herself. How absurd . . . and yet, for one moment, he had appeared like that in her imagination. She forced her eyes to tell the truth of the frayed sweater and thick duffle coat that he wore, the cord trousers and green rubber boots that had seen better days and the battered zipper bag that lay at his feet like a deflated balloon. He was only one of the fishing community . . . a long-shore fisherman back from selling lobsters or ordering equipment from one of the chandlers on the mainland.

As if sensing that he was being watched, he turned slightly and for a moment the dark jasper eyes looked into the wide green ones of the girl with the slightly pinched face. Dawn shivered, pulling her hat closer round her ears. It was cold out in the channel. She was aware of the dark gaze still on her. Had she shivered because she was cold, or was there something laser-sharp and penetrating that flashed between them? She bent to push her magazine back into the holdall with stiff fingers. She longed for a cup of hot coffee, but a glance at her watch told her that there was no time to go below to the small cafeteria before the boat docked.

The rustle of feet and gathered luggage grew as car passengers went down to the car deck and the foot passengers lined up as if they were about to leave a sinking ship. Dawn joined the line, recalling that taxis were not everywhere to be found in the small yachting harbour that was Yarmouth. The sun dipped its red hot globe into the sea and sank, leaving a pale grey and pink trail in the sky. It was going to be very cold if the wind sprung up, now that the sun had gone down. I was a fool not to bring gloves, thought Dawn. The handle of her larger bag was cold and slippery and her fingers barely closed over it. She hitched her holdall up round her neck so that she had two hands free for ticket and luggage, and hoped that all the cars wouldn't be gone, which would mean a wait of half an hour or more before one returned to scoop up any fares left on the quay.

Bert Cass passed close to her and muttered a greeting. She half smiled, but he felt no warmth and joined his friend, blocking her view of the gangway. A woman was arguing with the ticket collector and held up the line, but letting season ticket holders slip past with practised effrontery. Damn! thought Dawn. There goes the last taxi if

they get there first. She pushed forward as soon
as the others began to move and forgot the
slippery gangway. To retain her balance, she put
out a hand and the case fell over the side of the
gangway from her numb fingers. 'Oh!' she cried
in an agony that was part pain and part horror as
her case vanished from view. A sharp twinge ran
up her calf muscle and she hobbled to the side to
look over into the water.

'Fortunately, they thought of that. We get a
lot of numbskulls crossing here,' said a deep
voice. 'Ted . . . get a boat hook, will you?' called
the man with the dark hair. He regarded Dawn
coldly. 'Don't you know enough to keep a hold
on your bag?' She stared over at her bag, caught
up in a wire mesh that was strung beside the
gangway to catch falling articles, children or
dogs that might go over the barrier. Her relief
made her ignore the sarcasm and the frosty
glare. 'One of the men is coming. I can't wait . . .
I have better things to do than act as nursemaid
to you.'

Ted walked over, grinning. 'Dropped your
case, did you, Miss? Well, one good turn de-
serves another. Don't you remember? I came up
to your place last week and you dressed my arm a
treat.' He fished for the handle and skilfully
whisked the case back to safety.

'Thank you,' she said, with a brilliant smile.
'I'm glad there are *some* gentlemen on the Is-

land. When you come to us again, I'll put a pink
bow on your dressing!'

'Don't do that, Sister. My old woman would
think I was a poof.' He laughed. 'You look
shrammed. Get back to a nice hot cup of tea,
Miss.'

'I will as soon as I can, but I'll bet the last taxi
has gone.' She tightened her lips.

'Leg hurting, Miss? Don't look so surprised.
We all know you had a car accident. Nasty
things, cars.'

'Thank you again, Ted. See you soon.' She
walked slowly to the taxi rank and found that, as
she had expected, there were no cars there and
the man in the kiosk by the telephone told her
that one had gone as far as Newport, at least
twelve miles away, another was ordered to pick
up a party from Chale and the rest might be back
soon. She sat in the tiny bus shelter and shivered.
It was too far to walk and, in any case, her leg was
sore. Suppose the taxis didn't return? The man
in the kiosk was packing up for the night. There
was no reason why they should come as the last
boat was in and there wasn't another leaving for
the mainland tonight. I may have to stay in
Yarmouth for the night, she thought. That's ridiculous. The hospital was only about three miles
away and surely there would be some means of
reaching it? She thought longingly of Beatties
and the many people she could call on for help in

an emergency . . . even if all the taxis in London refused to drive her out to the hospital. A large tear formed and fell, leaving a salt trail down her cheek. I should never have come here, she thought bitterly. It's cold and unfriendly and if that oaf is any sort of an example of what the manners of the natives can be, I want to go away.

'Get in!' A curt voice broke into her thoughts. She stared at the huge black car that purred expectantly by the bus shelter. 'Come on, we haven't all night.'

'I'm waiting for a taxi,' she said, with dignity. 'It's very kind of you . . . I suppose you *are* offering me a lift? But I'd rather wait here.' Her teeth were chattering with cold and a sneaky wind whipped at the yellow hat.

'For God's sake get in. Do I *look* like Jack-the-Ripper? Where do you live? Hope it's this side of Newport, or you'll have to take a bus from there.' He thrust his head further through the open window. 'I warn you. There are no taxis . . . there are no other people willing to offer you a lift . . . I'm expecting a very important telephone call so I have no time to waste . . . and you are going to have pneumonia if you sit there much longer.' His tone became more gentle. 'Come on, I won't bite you and I'm far too busy to force my attentions on you, if that's what's worrying you. Not that I ever seduce girls with blue lipstick and cyanosed noses.' He held the door open on the passenger side and she meekly went round to get in, trying not to limp. 'Ted shouted about someone who couldn't walk home . . . so he was right and I don't have to scour the harbour for another legless wonder. That, at least, is a relief.'

'Are you always as rude as this?' asked Dawn. He glanced down at her and smiled for the first time. 'Do you know the St Boniface Hospital? I live in the third cottage from the main gate,' she said.

'Not far. I thought when you mentioned the hospital, you might be a runaway patient.' His tone was mocking but held more humour now.

'No, I just live in the cottage,' she said. And if he thinks I'm going to tell him anything about myself, he can think again, she decided.

The twilit hedges flew by and she relaxed in the warmth of the car. She flexed her hands and felt the circulation return. He put a hand over hers, briefly. 'Blue hands, too. You must be masochistic to cross the Solent in April without buttoning up. Just visiting? Ensnared by adverts that say "Come to the Sunshine Isle" and give good terms when it's snowing?'

'No, I've been here before. I do know the Island.' It was difficult to answer him politely. He had such a poor opinion of her and every word was a taunt . . . as if he wanted to goad her to rudeness. He was keeping her angry on purpose, but why? Was he so resentful of her being thrust on him by the nice warm-hearted man on the ferry that he had to take out his anger on her? She felt warmer and knew that the adrenalin was being stimulated by her own anger. Her fingers were soft again, although she was cold, and the uncontrollable shivering had stopped.

'I was in London today and it was quite warm there,' she said, defensively. 'I suppose that if you are out in this weather all the time, you *do* dress for it . . . or at least put warm clothes on when it's chilly.' She deliberately stressed the difference, showing that she noticed the frayed grubbiness of his clothes. She thought he laughed softly, but when she looked up, sharply, the dark eyes were watching the road and the full-lipped mouth was firm and still.

'This do?' he said and drew up by the main gate of the hospital.

'Thank you,' she said, and hesitated. He leaned across to open the door for her, not leaving his seat. He was driving a large and what must once have been an expensive car, but from his clothes he was a fisherman. She wondered if he expected a tip as he sat without moving, his hand across her lap holding the door slightly open.

'I never take money,' he said solemnly, reading her thoughts.

'Then, I'll say thank you again . . . it really was very kind,' she murmured, her colour rising. How embarrassing to think he guessed what was in her mind. He seemed to be holding the door, so that even with the rather draughty gap showing that she could go now, he wasn't really opening it any further. She put out her hand to push the door and it touched the lean brown hand that held the door fast. 'I can manage the door,' she said.

'Are you feeling warmer?' he said.

'I'm fine,' she said. 'I was cold, I admit, but it is warm in here and I'm nearly back to normal.' There was a moment of silence which she had to fill with words. The door was still only half open and she had the incredible impression that she was a prisoner.

'You have a little more colour. Tell me, were you very ill?'

'I'm not an invalid,' she said, crisply. 'And if you are so anxious about my health, Mr . . . er . . . if you think I should be in a warm atmosphere, I'd better get into the cottage as quickly as I can. I can make a hot drink and go to bed.'

'It sounds wonderful,' he said, and grinned, wickedly.

Her heart began to beat furiously. How dare he! 'If you'd just let me open the door, I can do just that,' she said.

'Ah . . . that's what I wanted . . . to see a little

more colour in your cheeks.' He chuckled. 'I imagine you might have quite a temper if you really let yourself go.' Her cheeks flamed and she was no longer in the least bit cold. She pushed the door and it flung open, nearly throwing her to the ground. 'Careful,' he said, calmly. 'You've forgotten something.'

She put her case on the pavement and reached inside the car for her shoulder bag. A pair of strong arms held her shoulders firmly and a pair of cool, firm lips planted a light kiss on her cheek. She grabbed her bag and backed away, tears of anger threatening to surface. 'You beast,' she said. 'How dare you?'

He shrugged and smiled, slightly. 'You were about to offer me a taxi fare . . . so I think that I took just enough for a three mile ride.'

'I'd rather pay you in money,' she grated. 'But if you took that as payment, let's make it quits. I owe you nothing. Goodnight . . . and I hope I never set eyes on you again.'

'I'll take you as far as Newport one day,' he laughed. 'That's at least four times further.' He was laughing at her, deliberately goading her into a hot temper . . . but why?

'For someone who has an important telephone call which makes you rush back to wherever you live, you seem to have all the time in the world,' she grated. 'Or is your telephone call the heavy breathing kind?' With as much co-ordination as she could manage with her throbbing leg muscle and the two pieces of luggage, she stumbled through the gateway to the cottage and fumbled for her key.

'Good Grief . . . I forgot the phone call.' The car reversed and sped away with a squeal of tyres, leaving Dawn helpless with rage and a kind of stormy elation . . . as if she was spent emotionally as well as physically, after an encounter that had annoyed her, stimulated her . . . and in a strange way, thrilled her.

Of the earth, earthy! she told herself. The overwhelming masculinity of the kind of man who worked with his hands and grew strong and full of animal attraction was not only found in books. There was beauty and grace in such men . . . as there was beauty and strength in a wild beast, but it didn't mean that she wanted to see him again. A shudder that was not from the cold but which had its beginnings in the suddenly erotic sensation of his remembered kiss on her cheeks made her drop her case in the tiny hall and rush to light the gas fire in the sitting room. Here was a haven . . . a place where she need never admit anyone she didn't wish to see.

She made coffee and a toasted sandwich, using some cheese and salami and tomatoes that she had brought with her from London, and as she sat on a huge floor cushion in front of the glow and thawed blissfully, she looked back into the shadows of the room and saw that they were sadly empty.

CHAPTER TWO

'Ouch! You really know where to prod, don't you, Irene?'

'You shouldn't go climbing mountains or whatever you got up to this weekend,' said Irene Meadows, the physiotherapist at the St Boniface cottage hospital.

'I didn't even climb Nelson's column. If you must know, it happened very much closer to home. I slipped on the gangplank on the ferry and twisted it again.' Dawn Campion looked worried. 'It doesn't mean staying off duty, does it? I am beginning to think I'll never be right again. I haven't been here for more than a few weeks on light duty, but surely I should be making more positive progress by now?'

'Nothing serious. It's only muscular and that isn't bad. I think you feel this more because it affected your Achilles tendon and put added strain on it. All the best footballers have it. I hope you didn't fall down and roll about, clutching your leg, as some of them do before walking away and playing again!' Irene massaged the leg gently. 'Or wasn't it worth it?' She laughed. 'For such histrionics, it isn't much fun unless there is an admiring and sympathetic audience to applaud you. The Lymington-Yarmouth ferry on a cold April evening couldn't have furnished you with much attention.'

Dawn bit her lip, not because the gently probing fingers hurt the sore muscles, but because she had a sudden vision of a dark head radiating hostility and disapproval at the silly girl who had let her luggage slip over the edge of the gangway.

'There were a couple of seagulls,' she said, 'and two men in fishermens' sweaters . . . one of them a patient here in outpatients, but I doubt if he was there when I fell. Most of the passengers had gone, bent on taking the taxis before any of the foreigners like me could get one.'

Irene stopped and looked up, aghast. 'You didn't *walk* back, did you? That's far too much for you at present. I think you can try the lower slopes of the Down next week, but three solid miles carrying luggage is too much, for a few more days,' she said, firmly.

'No, I didn't walk. I had a lift.'

'Oh, I wonder who that was. Did they give you names?' She laughed. 'I shall know more about it than you do when I go to the local.'

'I don't know his name, but he was one of the fishermen.'

'Funny . . . Bert Cass doesn't have a car and nor does his cousin, and if they were the only ones on the ferry, I doubt if you'd have seen any of the men from the boats at that time of day. They are usually stoking up with food for the night or drinking in the bar at the Smuggler's Rest before taking the boats out.'

'He was in blue sweater and duffle, with cords and wellies,' said Dawn.

'Fish scales under his fingernails and a strong smell of fish?' Irene laughed. 'It's diagnostic, my dear Watson!'

'No, he had very clean hands.' Dawn tensed and Irene looked up into her solemn face. 'He had beautifully manicured hands and he smelled of very good after-shave,' she said, in a kind of wonder. 'Why didn't it strike me as odd last night? I took one look at him and took it for granted that he was one of Bert Cass's fraternity.' She forced a laugh to hide her feelings. 'Now, Bert really does smell the part. We open the windows after he has his arm treated, but this man had working clothes that smelled more of the sea than of fish.'

'He might have been from the customs office or the coastguard station. Was he tall and fair?'

'He was tall . . . but dark and very bad tempered. He seemed intent on making me cross and was really very rude. I was glad to get out of the car and shut the cottage door behind me.'

'I can't think who that would be. If he offered you a lift, he couldn't have been all bad,' Irene paused, 'unless he thought you might be a girl alone who he could seduce. Not much talent for the local lads here until the tourists come with the first swallows.'

'He didn't want that . . . he said . . . that is . . .'

'What *did* he say? You're blushing, and you can't get away without telling me or I'll make you go off duty and stay in bed for a day,' she joked.

'He obviously didn't find me attractive. He made me get in the car, saying he wasn't Jack-the-Ripper and never seduced girls with blue lips and a cyanosed nose.'

'You were as cold as that?'

'I came away from London in full sunshine, feeling very warm, but cotton jeans and a zipper top aren't really ideal for the Solent in a cold wind. I was very cold.'

'And he made you react to him in some way . . . flirting with you would have been one way, but making you angry might be even better.' Irene was smiling. 'Dark, did you say? Driving a battered old Bentley?'

'How did you know?'

'That must be Dr Stratton, doing a locum for one of our GPs who is ill.'

'A *doctor*?'

'Who obviously thought you might be on the edge of hypothermia. The doctors here are very conscious of the condition. It would alert him at once to someone who was cold and numb and exposed to the elements. Most of the winter accidents here are complicated more by exposure and consequent hypothermia than by the injuries.'

'But I was only cold. I was walking about and alert and could go back to a warm cottage, hot drinks and bed.'

'He didn't know that, did he? It would have been possible for you to go indoors, feeling numb and cold but not worrying about it too much, feeling too tired to bother with a hot drink and going to bed inadequately covered and being quite ill.'

'Oh, come now, Irene. I've heard of it happening to elderly people living alone, but I'm not exactly old!'

'You have been ill . . . very ill,' said Irene, gently. 'With your hair scraped back under your nurse's cap and those shadows under your eyes, you look quite fragile. If you were cold and pinched as well, a doctor could well be worried.'

'He *did* touch my hand and say I was cold,' said Dawn. She wondered with a curiously sinking heart if the light kiss had been yet another way of testing her skin temperature! He was being therapeutic, raising her blood pressure and adrenalin flow by insulting her and goading her to react against him.

'When you two meet again, you'll laugh about this,' said Irene, comfortably.

'I doubt that very much. I think he was glad of the excuse to put me down. He didn't seem to be doing it as a therapy . . . more for kicks, I thought.' She laughed. 'And to think I accused him of being a heavy breather on the telephone.'

'Did he ring you up?'

'No . . . he was expecting a telephone call and when I was really angry, I said it was probably the heavy breathing type of call.' Irene nearly dropped the tube of cream she was squeezing. 'Well, how was I to know?' said Dawn, plaintively. 'But at least now I know who he is and he doesn't know me, so I might be able to avoid him in future.'

'Don't bank on it, he brings patients here.'

'You wouldn't give me away, would you?'

'No, of course not, but I think you'll like him when you meet again. He's one of my favourite people.'

'Why does everyone try to make friends for me? When I was at Beatties yesterday, my friend in casualty was trying to tell me that there was a man on the South coast who worked in London for a while who she wanted me to meet. I managed to stall her as I prefer to make my own friends, but here you are telling me I'd like your local monster . . . and I know the kind of man I like!' She laughed, but behind the laughter was a hint of sadness. He was not her type, but it was a blow to her pride that the kiss had not been spontaneous, only another means of annoying her.

'That's the lot,' Irene said. 'Come back tomorrow about ten and we'll try the cycling machine to stretch that tendon gently. You can have some heat instead of massage, too. Bring some shorts or a leotard . . . it's easier for a work-out and you have to get used to seeing that scar. You can go on duty, but take it easy.'

'Thanks, Irene, you're a gem.' Dawn pulled her thick tights on and caught a glimpse of her legs in the long mirror. There was nothing wrong with the shape of the long slim line and the scar would soon be almost invisible, but the thick tights were a protection behind which she could hide and refuse to admit the accident had happened. She could try to forget that Arnold had existed and be as she was before she met him.

'And, Dawn . . . buy some sheer tights. The men here need a bit of a thrill and there's nothing wrong with your appearance.' Irene gave a half smile. 'Come to terms and you'll forget it all in time, but you must make the next effort.'

'It's too cold for thin tights, and I'm going to buy thick jumbo cord trousers for off duty,' said Dawn, defiantly. 'I want to avoid being treated for hypothermia again.'

* * *

There were two men waiting in casualty when she went back. Bert Cass grinned as Dawn brought out his notes. 'Bit nippy on the ferry wasn't it, Sister?'

'Very. I had no idea it would be so cold,' she said, with a smile. The massage and treatment had made her leg feel fine and she was relaxed and warm.

'You look a bit different today,' he said with a hint of a leer.

'We all look better after a good night's rest and some hot food,' she said, crisply. 'Now, let me see that arm.' She peeled off the dressing and stared. 'What have you put on this skin?' The neat dressing that she had applied with soothing antibiotic cream and sterile gauze had gone and in its place was a soiled piece of linen smeared with an oily substance. Specks of sand adhered to the almost raw surface of the arm and a faint edge of inflammation surrounded the area.

'I think you'll have to see the doctor again,' she said. 'He'll be furious when he sees what you've put on here. It's petroleum jelly, isn't it?' He nodded. 'I suppose you also use it for putting on fish hooks to keep them from rust and other nice clean jobs like that?'

Bert flushed. 'How did you know?'

'I spent a lot of my time on the island, Bert. I went fishing and I helped with the gear. I'm not the complete ignorant overner.'

'You was last night. My cousin said he's seen warmer corpses on cliff ledges than you on that deck.'

'I'll clean this up and put on a sealed dressing. You should have a dressing that lets the air in but not infection, but if you lose it, what's the point?' She sighed. 'I suppose there's no hope of you keeping it dry?'

'Can't see how I can, Sister. We go out most nights now the weather is fair and the fish are there. Gets real mucky and wet on the boat and it's too late to come here for a dressing at four in the morning.'

'Have you tried? If Night Sister knew, she might help. It doesn't take long and it would make a lot of difference.'

'I could go crabbing for a spell. That's in the day and I could come back here late.'

'How late? The night staff would be too busy until after midnight when the wards settle down.'

'Oh, evenings, mostly. You could do my dressing and come down to the pub after.' He regarded her hopefully and she was reminded of the many times at the Princess Beatrice Hospital when similar suggestions had been made by patients. The rule there had been definite and final and was something that young nurses could use as an excuse. It was strictly forbidden to date a patient until they were not involved professionally. But those rules didn't apply in a small cottage hospital and certainly not for a sister.

'It's very nice of you,' Dawn said. 'I'd do your dressing if and when I was on duty in the evening, but my boy-friend wouldn't like it if I went to the pub with you.' She smiled, making him seem a threat to any man in love with her, and he lost the slightly sullen expression he had acquired when he saw that she would refuse him. 'We might see you there,' she lied, and he nodded and smiled. The dressing was firm and neat and Dawn made a note that Bert Cass should see the doctor as soon as convenient. She asked the junior nurse if she knew who was on call for Casualty. 'Is it Dr Tyley or Dr Hobart?'

'I think it's Dr Tyley after lunch, Sister. He said he was going to Bonchurch to test the waves this morning, but would look at anything we needed this afternoon.'

'When did you see him?'

'He telephoned when you were at Physio. I left the message on the pad in your office, Sister.'

'Thank you, Nurse. I'll write up the notes and make out the dispensary list for you to take down when you go to lunch. You're off duty this afternoon, aren't you?'

'It's my half day and I'm off tomorrow, Sister. Nurse Brody will be back after lunch.'

'Well, we've one more case in there. You dressed the abscess. Is it getting better? Less discharge?'

'Yes, Sister. It's nearly dry. I just put a dry dressing on as you said and he seems very pleased with himself. The last man came in when you were doing Bert Cass. I put some things in to boil, Sister.'

'What is it?'

'He's run a fish hook through the ball of his thumb. It's still in there and he's swearing!'

'Lay up and make sure there are some strong forceps that grip well. I'll see him and clean it up and see if it's something I can do.' She hesitated. 'There doesn't seem to be a doctor about, but I think he should have anti-tetanus serum unless he's had some lately.' She looked at the bare note-card that had just the name and address, age and occupation filled in.

'Mr Attril?' she said, with a smile at the patient.

'That's right, Sister. Can you get this bloody hook out? I tried, but it hurt too much.'

'I can see.' She turned the hand gently and saw that the hook had gone through the fleshy part of the thumb and the barb was through but resting in the skin as if Dave Attril had tried to tug it back the way that it had come, tearing against the barbed tip. She gently immersed the hand in a bowl of warm water to which was added some antiseptic lotion and the dirt and tension were washed away.

'That feels good . . . but it hasn't soaked out the hook, Sister.'

'It wasn't intended for that. I have to clean it up as well as I can and then remove the hook.' He paled visibly. 'Have you eaten lately?' He nodded. 'So you really shouldn't have an anaesthetic,' she said. 'If you think you'd rather wait for the doctor to put you under, it will have to be this afternoon. I can give you a pain killer, but I'd rather have that out as soon as possible. I promise it will come out clean and not hurt as much as you hurt yourself, trying to pull it back.'

He looked sheepish. 'It was a daft thing to do, Sister, but I thought I'd never get it out. Do what you like. I trust you.'

Dawn put on a gown and mask and lifted the cover of the tray that the casualty nurse had laid up. It was all there, the initial purifying lotion in a water base so that it wouldn't sting on application as a spirit-based lotion would do on the raw surfaces. She painted the surrounding skin and dribbled lotion over the protruding hook so that the wound was inundated. On the tray was a pair of wire cutters, boiled with the other instruments, and Dawn took them firmly in one hand while she held the patient's hand in the other. Nurse Fairbody, the casualty nurse, stood by and tried to keep his attention away from the towel-lined table on which his hand rested. Keeping the hook quite still and making no pressure, Dawn swiftly clipped away the end of the hook that bore the remains of the fishing line in the tiny ring at its end. She picked up the strong short forceps and locked them on to the barb. A short blast from the local anaesthetic spray making the area feel frozen came next and Dave Attril gasped at the sudden coldness. Dawn took a deep breath and with a continuous movement, drawing the hook in an arc along the line it had already taken through the thumb, she drew it out, bringing the clipped end through instead of pushing back the barbed hook.

Nurse Fairbody laughed. 'You can open your eyes now, Mr Attril. Sister has it out.'

He stared at the inflamed hole and a slow smile spread over his face. 'You're a ruddy marvel,' he said. He obediently sat with the hand soaking once more in clean lotion and Nurse Fairbody took a note of his temperature, pulse and respiration to make sure that there was no sign of infection.

'Have you had an ATS injection lately?' Dawn asked.

'In my coat. Get that black wallet out, Nurse.' He nodded towards his coat and Nurse Fairbody opened the shabby wallet. In it, wrapped in sealed plastic, was a card saying that Dave Attril had received an ATS injection within six months of the present accident. Another card stated his blood group and the fact that he was allergic to penicillin.

'This is very useful, Mr Attril, and it seems that you have no need for ATS. In fact, it would be dangerous to give it to you if you still have immunity. But why the sealed plastic case and the other details? You don't go round expecting trouble, do you?' She laughed and he smiled dryly.

'That's just what I do, Sister. I work on the boats but I'm also the coxswain of the lifeboat and we have to be ready for anything. We carry medical details in case of trouble. I have known it to matter,' he added simply.

'I see.' Sister Campion looked at him with respect. 'You do a great job, Mr Attril. I think we'll get away without infection, but come in tomorrow to have your temperature taken and we'll send a swab tomorrow if there is any discharge. Can't afford to take risks if you are allergic to penicillin. They would want to know what organisms are there and what to give you to treat infection if it should arise.'

'I think you know your job, too, Sister.' He watched her deft hands applying the dressing and smiled. 'Any time you like to walk up to the Smugglers, I'll buy you a drink.'

'That's the second invitation I've had today,' she said, and laughed. 'Do you all try to make alcoholics of your hospital staff?'

'Only the pretty ones with a bit on top,' he said. 'You'll do when it comes to the new service.'

'What do you mean?'

'Hasn't Dr Tyley told you? You must have heard of the chap from London who wants to add to the rescue service by ferrying accident cases by plane? They hope to set up a telephone link here for anything on the West Wight and one at Cowes for the other side of the Island.'

'Is it necessary? You have good hospitals here at Ryde and Newport and a long history of coping well with disasters at sea and on the cliffs.'

'Last time someone hit his head on the rocks, they flew a man in from East Grinstead to look at him as he needed special treatment, then they had to arrange an Air Sea Rescue helicopter to take them both back. There was too much delay and the man died. Sure, we cope with most things, but time is important when a casualty is exposed to the weather and the cold. You know that, Sister.'

Why did cold and exposure come into every conversation? 'Yes, you're right, of course,' she said. 'But I don't think I come into it.'

'You'd be surprised,' he said, and grinned. 'They'll be after you now we know you'll do.' He shrugged into his coat and waved from the door. 'Thanks . . . see you tomorrow.'

Dawn Campion washed the dirty instruments and gazed out of the window at the small white clouds scudding across a pure blue sky. The sun was brilliant, and on the common, birds were singing with all the ecstasy of spring and the air was warmer, if the attitude of the men talking on the corner was any guide. It seemed impossible that the wind could ever blow at gale force, that ships could founder on the bright coast or that anyone could die of the cold out there on the cliff ledges. She smiled. Dave Attril was still talking instead of going home to put his feet up after his experience. He was small and wiry and, she suspected, as tough as old rope. Her heart warmed to his no-nonsense approach to life and to his understated ability as a sailor and fisherman. I wonder what he means? . . . 'Now that you'll do', she thought.

She dried the instruments and turned the steriliser down as clouds of steam belched out, misting the windows between the sterilising room and the outer clinical room. She heard voices and saw vague shadows through the glass. Nurse Fairbody was over-enthusing as usual: 'It was the new sister who took it out, Doctor.'

'I met Dave Attril and he told me. Half the time, first-aiders who haven't learned their drill, or even trained staff who don't think, try to get the barb back the way it came. Dave said he was fool enough to try, which couldn't have made it easier for Sister.'

'She's very good, Doctor . . . but she trained in London,' said Nurse Fairbody, as if this described the Elysian Fields.

'So did I,' he said, in a conspiratorial whisper.

Dawn could resist it no longer. Carefully, she rubbed a tiny circle clear in the steamy window and peeped. She froze. Oh, no! It was impossible. The man who stood with Nurse Fairbody in the clinical room was dark and the jasper eyes smiled. Dr Stratton was dressed in smart but casual tweeds and a soft blue check shirt that added to the general air of rugged well-being.

'I don't know how she did it. I closed my eyes when she took up those forceps and I expected Mr Attril to jump off the table!' Nurse Fairbody was wide-eyed.

'It does take nerve if you aren't used to it, but a casualty sister meets all kinds of crises.' He laughed. 'Tell me; the cottages are used for staff here, aren't they?' She nodded. 'I thought so. I'm glad the new sister isn't as accident prone as one of your staff I met last night. I can't imagine her pulling a fish hook out of anything, or doing anything requiring strong nerve.'

'Who was that, Doctor? I didn't think we had any other new staff . . . but of course, she needn't be new. You haven't met us all yet, have you? You've been here only a week yourself with

Dr Hobart down the road, and you've been in here no more than three times.'

'She is a pale little thing with green eyes and very flat hair . . . and a limp. Might be secretarial, of course, in which case we shall be spared further disasters.' He walked to the door and then called back, 'I really came to ask if I could open an abscess this afternoon. Will you tell Sister or whoever is on duty, just the usual things,' he added, casually.

'Well, of all the cheek . . . I haven't got flat hair!' Dawn slammed down the steriliser lid over the set of instruments she had put on to boil and pulled the cord that set the air extractor working. 'I'm going to lunch, Nurse,' she called. 'I heard the doctor ask for a set and I've put it on to boil.'

The small dining room was cosy and looked more like the lounge of a small pub than the eating place for hospital staff. Bright floral curtains floated over the window ledges and the carpet was softly green. A good smell of well-cooked food came from the sideboard and Dawn helped herself to beef casserole and fresh vegetables.

'We do well for fresh fish and fresh vegetables,' said Irene, who had followed her into the dining room. 'Many of our patients may not say much, but they arrive with the most beautiful produce and thrust it at us as if it is of no value.'

She helped herself liberally and sat down with Dawn.

'The food is very good,' said Dawn, trying to forget the scathing tones of the man who had described her in such deriding terms.

'You look a bit hot and bothered. Been busy?' said Irene.

'A bit, but at least it makes life interesting.'

Irene looked at her sharply. 'I love living in the West Wight. I was over the moon when I got this job as it's conveniently near Francis.'

'Francis?'

'Didn't you know? I'm married to an aero-engineer who makes small planes. He commutes easily from here every day and I do what I want to do. You'll get to love it too. The only danger for you with a career to carve, is that you could love it too well and not want to leave.'

'If everyone was like you, and the ordinary patients I've met, it could happen, but so far I have yet to meet any members of the medical staff who come up to the standard of the ones I knew in London.'

'Someone has annoyed you badly. Be fair, you know you like Bruce Tyley and James Hobart. I know they are easy-going on the surface and don't seem to have many challenges to meet, but you just wait until you see them in action.'

'I'm sorry . . . I do like them. I was thinking of one man who has cropped up twice in the last

twenty-four hours, and each time I've liked him
. . . not at all.'

'Perhaps you haven't seen his best profile,'
said Irene, laughing. 'It isn't true . . . it can't be
true. He's been here for such a short time and all
the nurses and female patients are drooling over
him.'

'I hope they aren't disappointed. If every
other woman is mad about him, at least he will
not miss my adoration.'

'Oh, I don't know.' Irene saw the clear skin
flushed gently and the rich auburn hair curling
after the steamy theatre. 'He hasn't seen you on
duty, has he?'

'No.' Dawn shrugged. 'I'm chicken, Irene.
He's coming to open an abscess this afternoon. I
shall want to fall through the floor after the way
he spoke to me and knowing what he really
thinks of me.' She tried to smile. 'Nurse Brody
will be on duty. Perhaps I can ask her to assist,
and stay in the office until he's gone.'

'Not you. Go back and slay him. He's only a
man and you, believe it or not, are very much a
woman or you wouldn't be so upset when a man
insults you.'

'I'd love to do just that,' said Dawn, viciously.
'I'd like to slay him.'

She went to fetch some pudding and when she
came back to the table, a medical clerk was
talking to Irene.

'This is Sister Campion,' said Irene.

'I have a message for you, Sister. Nurse Brody rang through from Chale. She has a bad sore throat and her doctor insisted on taking a throat swab before letting her come back on duty. If her throat feels better tomorrow, he'll let her come back, but she will have to work on a medical ward until the swab is clear.'

'Oh, dear . . . that's terrible. I was hoping that she would be here for a case this afternoon.'

'Matron said that she will send an assistant nurse down to help clear up and to stay until Nurse Brody comes back.'

'Thank you,' said Dawn, weakly. She ate her pudding without tasting it and pushed away her plate.

'Cheer up,' said Irene. 'Nurse Peebles is very good. I keep telling her she should do general training and I think she might next year. You'll find her very useful . . . but you'll have to spell it out at first as she hasn't done any casualty.'

'You're trying to tell me that she can't scrub for anything or assist,' said Dawn, flatly.

'That's right, my pet. You have to brave the big bad wolf all on your own.' Irene chuckled. 'I'll have to organise my better half into arranging a get-together, new friends and old, all getting to know each other. Should be fun. You'll be here for Easter—what better occasion . . .'

She was still laughing when Dawn left the

room, to hurry back and make sure that there was no possible cause for Dr Stratton to find fault with anything.

CHAPTER THREE

'No NEED to panic, Nurse,' said Sister Dawn Campion, with a forced smile. 'I know you haven't been in this department, but if you follow instructions and keep away from anything sterile, we'll get along fine.'

'Thank you, Sister. I do want to work here, but at the moment I have butterflies in my stomach,' said Nurse Peebles.

Haven't we all, thought the new sister. She glanced at the closed door and wondered if she could bear to face the man who disliked her and would automatically consider her to be inefficient, or accident prone. 'If you'd put on a gown and mask, you can wait for the patient to come here. Make sure that he takes off any soiled outer clothing and clean him up if necessary.' From the few contacts she had made with the local fishermen, Dawn had learned that they arrived for treatment wearing their working clothes which usually consisted of very dirty salt-stained sweaters of oiled wool, thick trousers stiff with grease and heavy boots of service-weight rubber. Not all of them seemed to think it necessary to bathe very frequently and it was difficult to convince them tactfully that cleanliness was next to godliness!

'I think your job is easier than mine, then, Sister,' said Nurse Peebles. 'Have you ever tried to make a man have a bath when he thinks that all he needs is fresh air and sea water?'

'The very fact that he has an abscess on his shoulder points to a certain lack of hygiene, Nurse. If you have any trouble, call me and I'll see that he cleans up.' She thought of the working clothes of the man with dark hair and remembered the underlying cleanliness, the fragrance of clean masculinity and good after-shave, and decided that there was little excuse for anyone to be as smelly as Bert Cass.

The outer door swung open and the new sister felt her colour rising. This was ridiculous. It would be at least half an hour before Dr Stratton arrived . . . he might not come at all if Dr Tyley decided to come back in time to take the afternoon stint. She walked into the ante-room where there was a shower and sink for washing. The long white gown that she had tied tightly at the waist trailed slightly, making her hitch it up and bell it out over the belt. I'll have to look through the gowns and put to one side the smaller ones, she thought. This one would fit a giant. But there wasn't time to find another more suitable before the case arrived. The theatre cap was hardly better, needing a tuck at the back under the tapes of the white mask. At least my own grandmother wouldn't know me in this lot, she thought with a mixture of irritation and relief.

Even through the white mask, Dawn could smell the inevitable odour of fish and seaweed. She wrinkled her nose. The thickset man grinned nervously. 'Mr Carter?' Dawn asked.

'That's right, Sister.' He coughed slightly. 'Are you going to do me?'

She laughed. 'No, this is one for the doctor. He should be here soon, but first we must prepare you.'

'Oh, go on, Sister . . . you can do it. Dave says you're a real dab hand at it.'

'Mr Attril said that?'

'He came straight down to the Smugglers and showed us what you did.'

'He didn't take the dressing off?' She was appalled.

'No, but he told us how you got it out without hurting. Can't you put some of that cold stuff on and lance it a bit?'

'Sorry . . . I'd do it if there was no doctor here and if it was an emergency, but you've had this for some days now and half an hour won't make any difference.'

'Is it Dr Tyley?'

'I doubt it. He was held up with another appointment,' she said, wondering how many times Bruce Tyley stayed riding the surf in a wet-suit when he should be on duty.

'Dr Stratton?' His face cleared. 'I don't mind him, but Tyley is a bit of a butcher.'

'You've met Dr Stratton?'

'Yes, but not in here. One of the lads told us about him. He's good,' he added, with conviction.

Dawn Campion smiled. Was a reputation made or broken in this small community just by word-of-mouth praise or condemnation? Perhaps her notoriety as a numbskull would spread also and her patients would filter away to more efficient places for treatment. It might be interesting to see the two factions of opinion. Dr Stratton with his pre-conceived ideas of her worthlessness and the glowing reports that Dave Attril was broadcasting in the Smugglers Rest.

'First things first,' she said crisply. 'That sweater will have to come off and anything you may be wearing under it. Then Nurse will swab the area to make sure it is clean before the doctor comes.'

She went back to lay up the trolley with a scalpel and probes, dissectors and scissors of various lengths and thicknesses, together with forceps, sponge holders and a selection of rubber drains and corrugated rubber in case the abscess was deep and needed to have the opening kept apart so that all infected discharge could drain before healing began. The danger was that if the surface healed over before everything had drained away, a pocket of infection might be left behind which would spark off another abscess later when the course of protective antibiotics was finished.

'Sister?'

'What is it, Nurse?'

'I've taken his sweater off and his vest, but he has filthy hair and his neck could grow potatoes.' Nurse Peebles sighed. 'He says he never washes his hair until the weather is warmer . . . but he must get it wet all the time out in the boats! Says he'll catch his death.'

Mike Carter sat with a large towel over his shoulders in the warm room. He looked powerful and rather forbidding, but his smile was fleeting and nervous.

'Come on, now, we'll have to get you nice and clean for the doctor,' said Sister Campion. 'I think you should have a shower. It will save time and you'll feel good after it.' She looked down at the sandy boots. 'Help him off with the boots, Nurse.'

Nurse Peebles dragged off the heavy boots and the smell of salt and sweat and stale socks rose to greet her nostrils. 'Phew!' she said.

'They get a bit strong,' he said.

'I really think you'll have to shower. Your hair might well be the reason for the abscess being as bad as it is. Dirt and grease from your hair could fall on your shoulders and enter any open wound.' Dawn went over and examined the inflamed area on his right shoulder. It was quite extensive and was at the base of a half-healed cut that ran from shoulder tip to the end of his shoulder blade. 'I wonder if Dr Stratton will want to take you to the main theatre and give you anaesthetic,' she said, more to herself than to the patient.

'I don't want gas . . . I had it for a tooth and I was sick,' he said, firmly.

'It's a very nasty place,' she said. 'Have you had anything to eat lately?'

'I had three nice fresh dabs and half a loaf with a couple of beers before we came off the boat.'

'Didn't anyone tell you yesterday that you might have an anaesthetic?'

He looked defensive. 'Came off the boat, Miss, I mean, Sister. Had to have something, didn't I, before we docked? It's hungry work fishing the bay.'

'I can sympathise, but it does mean you'll have to have a local anaesthetic. Have we got your full address? Can you go somewhere near to rest after the treatment?'

'That's my mother's address at Chale. I'm on the boat more times than not, but I can go to Dave's and put my feet up for an hour, like I do when we think we're for life-boat call.'

'You help with that, too?'

'It makes a change,' he said, with a laconic shrug. She smiled. He dismissed life-boat service as something necessary to be done with no fuss, but he couldn't face an anaesthetic. 'I could have a bit of a wash. There's no call for washing my hair is there, Sister?'

'I'm afraid so, Mr Carter. You can strip off in there and you'll find plenty of soap and a scrubbing brush in the shower cubicle.'

'I can't manage on my own,' he said with an innocent smile. He glanced at Nurse Peebles who blushed pink. 'Honest, Sister, I need some help.'

'Very well, if you go in there and strip, I'll send someone to help you.' He went in with such alacrity that it was almost as if he welcomed a bath. 'Nurse,' said Sister Campion in a low voice, 'fetch the porter and ask him to help for five minutes.'

Nurse Peebles giggled and ran into the corridor, returning a minute later with a grinning porter, already rolling up his sleeves. 'Careful with his shoulder,' warned Dawn, 'but there's nothing wrong with his head or his feet. Both need a good wash before the doctor sees him.' She turned to the laughing nurse. 'Is there a hospital set of pyjamas we could have . . . and a dressing gown? He can't put that smelly jersey on before it's washed or until we find a clean shirt for him to wear under it.' Once more the nurse went on her errands and Dawn smiled as she listened to the cries of offended pride coming from the cubicle.

'What shall I put on him, Sister?' the porter called.

'Here you are . . . he can't wear his out-door things yet or he'll infect the wound when the abscess is opened.' She handed in the bright blue pyjamas and dressing gown and a few minutes later a subdued but clean man emerged from the cubicle, a towel wrapped round his damp head. He wore the flat mules that he found in the pocket of the dressing gown and his blue eyes were wary.

'I didn't reckon on this,' he said.

'Go on, you'll have all the girls after you now you smell nice,' said the porter. 'Is that all, Sister? I thought I saw Dr Stratton's car coming.'

She tried to sound unconcerned. 'Thank you for your help,' she said. 'If you see him, tell Dr Stratton that we're ready.'

'It was a pleasure, Sister.' The door opened and in strode Dr Stratton. 'They're all ready, Sir, and Mike had a bit of a wash for you,' said the porter as he left, grinning all over his face.

'Good God! That can't be Mike Carter,' said Dr Stratton. Mike grinned, sheepishly. 'Are we all ready? I haven't much time, Nurse Brody.'

Dawn relaxed. If he thought she was the staff

nurse, it was all to the good, and for reply she wheeled in the trolley.

'Get him lying on his face, will you. I'll scrub,' he said.

The two young women settled the large muscular body on the table with pillows under his stomach and ankles to take the strain and make him as comfortable as possible while the treatment was being done. He was stripped to the waist and knew that he looked good. Nurse Peebles seemed impressed by his physique, but as Dawn Campion glanced into the scrubbing-up bay and saw the strong shoulders and clear skin of the man standing there, also stripped to the waist, she saw the difference between animal strength of an ox-like variety and the supple, equally strong but more delicately constructed panther-like muscles, of the doctor. A fine fuzz of dark hair covered his chest and ran down in a faint line to disappear below his waistline. A fleck of soap splashed up and dewed his shoulder where a dark mole pinpointed the ripple of his biceps, and she wanted to smooth it away . . . to take a towel and caressingly dry the damp flesh.

She turned away, appalled at her fantasy. She handed him a sterile gown and stood silently while he shrugged into it, then tied the back tapes securely. He slipped on size seven and a half gloves . . . how had she known so certainly without checking that he would wear that size?

She had only the slight contact on her hand in the car and the sight of the lean brown hand on the car door to tell her that his hands were beautiful, strong, powerful . . . and gentle.

'How did you do this, and why haven't you come in to be treated?' he asked the patient.

'Some fool threw a net over without freeing it and I grabbed it to unsnarl it. The twine cut down into my shoulder and ripped it open.'

'When was this?'

'Week before last. It got sore, but it closed up and I thought it was okay. I've good healing flesh. We all have,' he boasted. 'All except my grandad. He died of blood poisoning. Got a rusty hook stuck in him,' he added, with evident satisfaction.

'And that's what will happen to you if you do this very often. I suppose you pulled on a filthy jersey and went on fishing?'

'Got no nice girl to wash my things of me, have I, Nurse?' he said to Nurse Peebles, his blue eyes snapping with laughter. 'I'm open to offers.'

'Well, someone cleaned you up nicely,' said Dr Stratton. 'Can I have a spray, Nurse? Two bursts and then rest, then one more, I think.' He was busily swabbing the area round the abscess with antiseptic dye. Sister Campion sprayed and the patient winced, then relaxed. Dr Stratton took the scalpel and drew it lightly across the tense swelling. 'I can't believe it's true,' he said, calmly. 'Who cleaned you up and made you have a bath? Now you know what happens to men who neglect septic wounds. They have the fury of the nursing staff unleashed on them!' All the time, he was swabbing and draining and probing gently, so that Mike listened and seemed to feel little pain.

'It was the new sister. One look from those eyes and I turned to jelly, Doctor,' said Mike. He turned his head slightly on the pillow and saw the soiled and bloody swabs on the tray. He turned a pale greeny-grey and fainted.

'I hope that your presence didn't make him pass out, Sister . . . I'm sorry, I didn't know that it wasn't Nurse Brody,' he said, calmly. Sister Campion felt the pulse of the patient, put his head to one side to make sure that his airway was clear, and stood by the head of the table to watch his colour. She nodded, as if pre-occupied with her patient, and didn't reply. Dr Stratton probed more deeply and inserted a piece of corrugated rubber along the length of the incision. He reached for a the needle holder with the needle and nylon suture already attached and grunted his satisfaction. 'Good . . . I can stitch now that he can't feel it . . . I think there's just time for two more stitches . . . there.'

Mike groaned and tried to edge away from the needle, but he was still half asleep. 'Gather up the swabs, Nurse, and clear them away . . . and cover the dirty instruments before he sees them. We don't want him passing out again,' said Sister Campion, forgetting everything but the well-being of her patient. As Mike groaned again and tried to sit up, there was nothing on the trolley or floor that could upset his equilibrium. A dressing was stuck on securely and a padded dressing added to make it more comfortable when he was lying down and also to absorb the expected discharge from the drainage incision.

'You'll have to stay in for a few hours, Mike. I had to put in a drain and we can't have you rubbing against something on the boat and dragging it out. I also think you need a course of antibiotics to be quite sure we've clobbered it.' Mike twisted round, grimacing, slightly. 'It will be stiff for a while, but I'll ask Sister on the ward to give you a painkiller.' He looked at the clock. 'Can I leave it to you, Sister? I have an appointment and I'm late.' He tore off his mask and gown and hurried into the changing room. He appeared almost immediately, dressed with his briefcase in his hand. 'Thank you very much,' he said, formally. 'By the way, we haven't been introduced. I'm Miles Stratton, in practice down the road for a few months and a kind of enforced honorary surgeon-cum-dogsbody here for anything that crops up when the casualty officer is away.'

'I am Sister Campion,' she said, coolly, but

didn't remove her mask. He hesitated, stared at her briefly and hurried away, wearing a slightly puzzled frown.

'You didn't give him much encouragement, Sister,' said Nurse Peebles.

'I saw no need,' said Dawn, sharply. She smiled. 'But you should talk—be careful of Mike Carter. He doesn't need *any* encouragement by the look of him.'

'He's a big hunk of muscle,' said Nurse Peebles, 'But quite nice with it.'

'He'll be asking you out . . . how's your rating at this legendary Smugglers Rest? I believe it is a throbbing centre of gossip.'

'Who said the Smugglers?' said Mike as they wheeled him to the ward in a wheel chair. 'I'll stand you both a drink when I'm out.'

The two girls laughed. 'That's three drinks I'm owed today,' said Dawn. She told Nurse Peebles to go back and clear the theatre while she passed on the messages about Mike Carter. 'Be very careful with the swabs and instruments. You haven't any open cuts on your hands have you? I think after a case like this you should wear gloves while you clear up and plenty of disinfectant. That discharge looked pretty lethal.'

The department was almost back to normal when she went back to help clear the instruments. The ward nurse had put Mike to bed in spite of his protest that all he needed was a good sit-down and a pint at the local to buck him up a bit. He suffered the indignity of an injection of antibiotic and accepted the painkiller meekly, showing that he was in more pain than he liked to admit. As Sister Campion glanced back to his bed, he was already drowsing, and she smiled as she put the instruments on to boil. Such a tough man, but so weak when it came to the knife.

She dried the hot metal and laid the instruments back in the cupboard. Were all strong men cowards at heart? Would Dr Stratton be the same under stress? She imagined the strong features, the cleft chin and the turbulent hair, and pushed the soiled linen into the bag with unnecessary force. He had dominated the department. As soon as he appeared, he was the one who was important. She shrugged. He's a big fish in a tiny pond, she thought, and tried to dismiss him from her thoughts. She tried to think of him within the context of Beatties, the hospital where she had trained, and was forced to admit to herself that he compared with any of the handsome, strong and intelligent men she had met there. A big fish in a small pond, she told herself again, without too much conviction. The steriliser boiled over and she hurriedly switched it off.

If I had taken off my mask, would he have recognised me? she thought. Perhaps he will never link the sister who had everything ready for him, and made Mike have a bath, with the girl with the pale face, smudgy eyes . . . and the flat hair. She giggled. He must have meant the yellow hat. It had never been a favourite possession, but as an aunt had knitted it for her, she had put it in the pocket of her blouson jacket to wear in case of rain. He thinks I have green eyes and yellow flat hair, I suppose. He can't have seen a single strand of my hair and so he used his very dodgy imagination. The idea gave her confidence. If he saw her, dry and relaxed, with colour in her cheeks and her hair a riot of auburn beauty, he might well forget the girl he despised and see only the new sister who was cool but efficient.

She hummed a tune as she put away the swab drums that came up from the autoclave and looked forward to the evening when she was off duty but on call until the night staff came on duty. Nurse Peebles made tea and produced some sticky buns that would add inches to even the slimmest hips if taken as a normal diet but which were irresistible as an occasional treat. With her tea cup half-way to her lips, Dawn heard a man's voice outside the door. She heard the slower tones of the porter telling him that there was nothing happening in Casualty and she braced herself to meet whoever it might be with that deep voice and an air of authority.

'That sounds like Dr Tyley,' said Nurse Peebles. She whisked the buns back into the tin. 'If he sees them, he'll eat the lot,' she said and put them away, bringing out the hospital issue of plain biscuits. Dawn hid a smile as the door opened and he walked in, looking round and then staring at the tea pot. 'Would you like a cup of tea, Dr Tyley?' said Nurse Peebles.

'What a well-regulated department,' he said. 'All cases cleared by the time I come back and tea made.'

'Have a biscuit,' said Nurse Peebles.

He accepted one without enthusiasm. 'I'm hungry . . . haven't you anything better to offer a poor, tired doctor?'

'It depends what made you tired,' said Dawn. She had met him only twice but found him amusing and easy to talk to.

'I was battling against the elements for two hours,' he said, impressively.

Dawn looked out at the clear sky and the gently swaying trees. 'I thought the gale died last night,' she said. 'But didn't I hear somewhere that Dr Tyley disappeared this morning with a wet-suit in his car, bound for the surf at Horseshoe Bay?'

He nodded, sadly, with a gleam of amusement in his eyes. 'All in the cause of science,' he said.

She ignored the warmth growing in the bright blue eyes and half turned away to drink her tea. 'Doctors who make others do their work buy their own buns, is that the rule of the house, or isn't it, Nurse?'

'That's the rule of the house, Sister.'

'In that case, I shall dunk my biscuit and pretend that I like it.' He dipped the biscuit into his tea and Nurse Peebles giggled. 'I really came with a proposition, Sister.' The two girls looked cautious. Gossip had it that Dr Bruce Tyley was a woman chaser and tried his luck with every presentable newcomer to the hospital, but he was attractive and Dawn couldn't conceal the dimple that appeared in her cheek when she tried not to smile. He drank deeply and handed the cup back for more tea. 'I expect you've heard about the new service?'

'The voluntary air ambulance? I heard about it in a roundabout way, but I hadn't heard that anything definite was decided.'

'It's been discussed and several local business men with private planes have put their names down as volunteer pilots. We want to relieve Air Sea Rescue of the more run-of-the-mill accidents on land and leave the clever stuff at sea to them. It could be fun,' he added.

'Fun for the pilots?'

'Fun for all the volunteers. How do you fancy yourself as a Flying Sister?'

'You make me sound like a pantomime fairy on a wire,' said Dawn.

'I'm serious. We want volunteers who have

had casualty experience from all the hospitals, to fly with the patients if a doctor isn't there, or with a properly equipped air ambulance that we hope to buy from voluntary subscription, in the event of a disaster.'

His face had changed from the slightly effete but charming expression to one of intense commitment. In a way, he's like the fishermen, thought Dawn. They joke about the serious business of rescue and yet it means a lot to them.

'I don't see how I could help,' she said. 'I don't know how I'd react to such conditions.'

'From what I hear, you're just the girl we need.'

'And who told you that?'

'A few very satisfied patients and members of staff.'

'Oh, I suppose that Dave Attril has been talking in the Smugglers.'

'He might well have done, but I was thinking of Mike Carter.' He laughed. 'Anyone who can make that man bare his body in a shower must be dynamite.'

'You're mistaken,' said Dawn. 'It was all done under false pretences. He thought I was going to send Nurse Peebles in to bath him . . . but we thought that it would be more seemly to ask the porter to do it.'

They laughed, but Dawn was increasingly aware of the appraisal in his eyes. She was glad that she had not had time to buy thinner tights as Irene had suggested, not because she was afraid of him seeing her scar but because she knew that even scarred, her legs were long and shapely and that black stockings were sensual garments, when they covered legs with a dark alluring film. I could wear ordinary tights, she thought, but it had been traditional at Beatties for all staff to wear the same colour, and far from black stockings being the dull uninteresting underpinnings that the original uniform demanded in Queen Victoria's time, to prevent the male patients from becoming inflamed, thin nylons were both practical and attractive under short dresses, and anything but dull!

'But I work here,' she said. 'When would you want volunteers? Would it mean staying up at night? That would be fine in an emergency, but it wouldn't be fair to busy staff to make them do that as a general rule.'

'Any volunteer would put her name down against her off-duty time, say once or twice a week, when she knew she would be within call . . . say you had an evening off and were taken out to dinner, you could leave a telephone number and come back in a hurry or report to the scene of the accident as soon as you were alerted.'

'What about equipment?'

'We haven't worked that out yet, but I think

each person should have a basic first-aid kit with dressings, painkillers and tourniquets . . . eye pads . . . a few things like that, and this should be kept in a waterproof bag and be carried at all times the volunteer might be needed.

'It sounds a very sensible idea. Did you think of it?'

'I'm afraid I can't claim all the fame. Miles Stratton thought it up and when he came here, I promised to help arrange the Island link.'

'Dr Stratton?' Her mind was in a whirl. She had had a growing uneasy conviction that he was the friend of Irene Meadows, the casualty sister at Beatties.

'Yes, he is very keen. He has a pilot's licence and has access to a small plane based on the Island, and would tell other pilots what to expect. He's due to join the RAF in the autumn and he wants to get the servvice started before he goes.'

'That means he'll leave the Island?'

'He says he'll make it his base and come back when his leave allows.'

'What of his family?'

'Oh, I expect when he gets married his wife will have something to say about where they live, but until that happens, he's fairly free, I think.'

'I don't think I'd be suitable,' said Dawn. 'I haven't flown in a small plane and I'm not keen to try.'

'You don't have to fly the thing yourself, silly.'

'I know that . . . but I might object to working with amateur pilots.'

'They all have licences. There's no need to worry about that.'

'I'm sure you're right,' said Dawn, but her mind wanted to scream that she couldn't bear to be in a small plane with a patient and the one man who could reduce her to a quivering mass of inhibition.

'Talking of the Smugglers Arms,' he said.

'Who was talking of that place?'

'Everyone sooner or later gravitates there. If you haven't breathed the thick smoke of the bar, you haven't lived, and if you haven't sampled the more rarified atmosphere of the snack bar, you have never eaten Ambrosia or whatever is the dish of the evening.'

'I'll get there one day,' said Dawn. Nurse Peebles gathered up the cups and tea pot and took them to the sink to wash up. Bruce Tyley settled down in his chair.

'Haven't you a round to do?' asked Dawn. 'I don't think Dr Stratton will do it for you. He left in a hurry with a briefcase and said he was late for an appointment.'

He rose to his feet and stretched. 'You're right, Sheila,' he said, with an exaggerated Australian accent.

'Ah, I was wondering about that. Not much

trace of an accent, but it's there. What made you leave Aussie land?'

'Chased out by the women,' he said. 'They all adore me and I just couldn't take it.'

'The original male Australian chauvinist?'

'Not a bit of it. I even let women pay their rounds when I take them out.'

'Great!' said Dawn.

'Which reminds me. I *am* hungry and you are off tonight. I think it's my duty to introduce you to the bright lights and the music of this exclusive resort.'

'What bright lights?'

'There's a lamp post outside the Smugglers and one down by the harbour! but there will be really good fish to eat and . . . I'd like to take you out to dinner.'

'And the music? I must have music.'

'Dave Attril plays a crafty accordian when he's drunk enough, and the songs get fruitier as the night goes on.'

'I ought to . . .'

'If you say you have to wash your hair, I shall know that I have completely lost my touch and I shall jump off the pier.'

'I couldn't sleep if I thought you had done that so I suppose I'd better prevent a tragedy,' she said, her green eyes sparkling. 'Go and do your round and meet me at the third cottage at seven.'

'I know where you live,' he said.

CHAPTER FOUR

'IT ISN'T as badly lit as that.' Bruce Tyley looked at the large torch that Dawn was carrying as they walked down the garden path from her small cottage. 'Perhaps we haven't a respectable casualty sister in our midst!'

'How does a torch make me suspect?' she said.

'You might be planning a wreck as they did on these shores long ago.'

'How could a torch make a wreck? Have you been to the Smugglers already?' It was good to respond to his banter. 'Explain, please, Doctor.'

'Surely you've heard of the wreckers who set up lights on the rocks to lure ships to their doom? They either set up torches so that ships thought they were looking at harbour lights, or drove cattle over the rocks with lamps swinging from their necks.'

Dawn shivered. 'I've read about it and when I came here in my school days, I was fascinated by the pictures and remains of wrecks on view at Blackgang Chine.'

'Blackgang? I thought that was just for the tourists?'

'There's a lot of that sort of thing too, distor-

ting mirrors and slot machines, electronic games
. . . I wonder if they have one with wrecks now?'
She laughed. 'It's a curious mixture. Just when
you think it's a load of touristy rubbish, you turn
a corner and the sheer beauty of the Chine takes
your breath away. The views are fantastic and
it's easy to see how smugglers thrived among the
rocky clefts and the deep caves in the cliffs. The
relics at the top in the museum are good and
many people go there without bothering with the
other side of the place.'

'I haven't been there. I think the advertise-
ments are off-putting.' He bent sideways and
she could see the glint in his blue eyes. 'You'll
have to take me there one day . . . in case I get
lost.'

They came to the uneven road leading to the
Smugglers Rest, and Dawn switched on her
torch, shining it on the ground in front of her. 'I
thought it might be tricky away from the road,'
she said.

'I would have thought that you would be as
nimble as a Koala bear . . . but perhaps I was
misled by your cuddliness.'

'I don't know much about them, but I believe
that Koala bears bite! I thought that everyone
knew about my limp,' she said, with an attempt
at lightness.

'I heard, but it isn't noticeable. When you
forget about it, you walk normally. You just lack

confidence. You need a strong arm round you
. . . like this.'

'I can manage better with the torch,' she said,
and shrugged his arm away.

'I was right,' he said, with mock solemnity.
'The woman is a wrecker. She lures men out at
the end of a torch and makes them feel protective
. . . concerned and very much attracted . . . to
the light in your eyes.'

'I only ask for a safe passage, sir,' she said.

'And yet, every time you glance at me in this
infuriating dim light, I receive the green light.'

'I can't help the colour of my eyes,' she said. 'I
can only tell you that they never give signals of
that sort . . . to any man.'

'You intrigue me, Sister dear . . . but more of
that later. The hostelry is a blaze of light and you
can gain sanctuary there.' He laughed. 'I don't
even know your name, so I can't expect any
favours from a strange woman. Let's start again.
I'm Bruce and you are . . . ?'

'Dawn. I can't think how I came by a name like
that. My mother was a sentimental creature, I
believe; not that I remember much about her, as
she died when my brother was born. She was
immersed in Homer and the ancient Greeks at
the time, or so my father told me. She saw me, all
red-faced and squealing, and as you know,
babies curl their fingers round anything they
touch. She saw them gripping her hand and said

they were like the rosy-fingered dawn that Homer spoke of so often . . . so I became Dawn.'

'I think that's rather good . . . but I'm sure you never squealed.'

'I still do if I lose my temper,' she said, in a half-warning tone.

They walked to the back of the pub to the small restaurant and were shown to a table by the window overlooking the sea. From the west the sky was stroked with pastel clouds in mares' tails against the turquoise distance. A sailing boat shook out red sails and was urged down the tide by a light wind and from the shore came the slow pull of waves on shingle. 'It's good here,' said Bruce.

'It all looks so innocent. Just the flat sea and a few boats and the sea birds. It's difficult to imagine a dark night with the wind howling and a ship in distress being pounded on the rocks round the Needles.' She paled. 'If they have this rescue service, they would be called out at any time . . . even in the dark.' She gazed at him with huge eyes. 'They must be very brave people. I don't think I could do it.'

'You could bring your torch,' he said, and patted her hand on the table. 'Come on, let's order . . . I'm famished.'

After London, with its many restaurants, wine bars and bistros, Dawn had expected very little from such a small inn in a tiny village, but it became apparent that the Smugglers Rest was widely known and had an excellent reputation. The residents of the Island were glad to be able to use their own amenities while the visitors were still slogging away to earn their holiday money to spend later, when the schools released the children who would swarm over the beaches and foreshores, blissfully searching for shells, digging sand castles in the golden sands and fishing for small fry in the shallows, in the warmer days of summer.

The locally caught fish were delicious, served with care in a delicate sauce and accompanied by salads and fresh locally grown vegetables. Bruce chose an Australian wine that was dry and quite adequate as a table wine, and as they ate, they talked little, but enjoyed the ambience of the place, the gentle murmur of voices from the bar on the other side of the wall and the soft red lamp-light on the small tables.

'You must try their apple pie.' Bruce ordered for her in spite of her protest that she would sink without trace if she fell in the bay, and Dawn found that she could finish her helping, huge though it was and smothered with fresh cream.

'There . . . you don't know what you can do if you try,' said Bruce.

'There's some difference between eating a huge meal in lovely surroundings and helping save lives on a windy cliff top,' she said.

'Tell me about your accident,' he said.

'No.' To her own surprise, she found that she couldn't talk about it to Bruce. 'I want to forget it. It was unfortunate and it's over . . . and I can walk again.' She changed the subject. 'Irene has helped a lot. You know her, I believe. I haven't met her husband yet, but he sounds nice.'

'He's great. He was the first to offer the use of his plane for the service and his firm is adapting an old plane to take two stretcher cases. He said that it is ready for use at any time, although the interior fittings are only basic as yet.'

'You'd need to keep it basic, wouldn't you? Whoever travels in it will want all the room possible to move about if there is much to do for the patient.'

'What do you think you'd need?'

'The stretchers, a locker for blankets and pillows, some kind of heating and the means to boil water . . . somewhere to store drugs and syringes and a large first-aid box with a good assortment of dressings and a pack of sterile instruments . . .' She stopped when she saw his smile. 'You know . . . the bare bones of emergency treatment with no frills. Oxygen . . . you'd need that.'

He sipped lazily at his coffee. 'You're good . . . you know that? You just need educating and self-confidence.'

She shook her head. 'I'm all right if I know what is expected of me, but there are still some people who can reduce me to jelly if they are sarcastic or unfair. I couldn't work with people I didn't know, especially if I wasn't sure of their efficiency.'

'You sound like Miles. He said almost the same when we were talking about it. He insisted that all the staff who volunteered should be hand picked. He doesn't want empty-headed girls going along for the ride and the kudos . . . and the doubtful thrill of being with a gorgeous hunk of manhood like me.'

'He said the last bit . . . meaning him or you?' Dawn found that she became uneasy whenever that man's name was mentioned, and her only protection was in flippancy.

'Me, of course, unless you like the dark and moody types?'

'He isn't my idea of a cosy companion,' she said. 'I don't think we'd get on very well if we had to work in those conditions.'

'You've met him in Cas?'

'Oh, yes . . . that was easy, but it was only a simple incision of abscess on Mike Carter. He wasn't there for more than half an hour, and we hardly spoke to each other.'

Bruce raised one eyebrow incredulously. 'My, my, Miles must be losing his touch. Most of the nurses grovel before him.' He chuckled. 'I must make quite sure that he knows that you let me take you to dinner.'

'Oh, *no*! Don't do that.'

He stared in surprise. 'Why not? It's a feather in my cap, I can tell you. He beat me to it with one very nice dish from the aero-engine factory and I don't like to be bested.'

'It's just that I dislike him and would rather you didn't make him notice me. I can't help on this emergency service, so it doesn't matter if he thinks I'm a . . . numbskull.' She laughed a little desperately. 'I'd rather not get to know him.'

'Fine. All the better. It might annoy the old boy to think there was one woman who didn't drool over him. It makes my claim more secure.' He leaned forward. 'And I think I do want to make a claim,' he said, with meaning. 'You are the prettiest woman we've had here since I came.'

'And I've heard that you are an authority on such matters, Bruce,' she said, dryly.

'Lies, all lies,' he said, but flushed slightly. 'It's been a long hard winter and there isn't much to do here except gossip and tear apart the reputations of one's so-called friends.'

'Whatever the reason, I'd rather not be added to the list of people deserving gossip,' she said, in a low voice. 'I wasn't just hurt physically, Bruce. Some scars go deeper and I'm off men for the present.'

He took her hands across the small table and the rosy light fell on her slender wrists with the lace edge of her frilled shirt adding to the illusion of delicacy. He kissed the pulse beat on her wrist before gently releasing his grip. 'I get the message . . . but let me be around when spring comes, Dawn.'

The soft light and the sensation of well-being after a good meal in relaxed surroundings lessened her resolution. 'You're the nicest man I've met for a very long time,' she said. The hand that still lay on the white table cloth was seized again with more force and considerable fervour. 'No, Bruce,' she said, 'That wasn't a come-on. I just like you very much, that's all.'

Her face was faintly flushed and the auburn hair glowed like a warm beacon above her flawless brow. The soft warm shirt of fine wool, trimmed with a froth of lace under the velvet waistcoat, was like something out of a romantic novel and the man who came to the entrance of the crowded dining room and looked round for a table, stared and failed to hear the waiter say that there would be a table free in five minutes if he would give them time to clear and re-lay one that had just been vacated.

'You have no right to burst into my life looking like that,' Bruce said. He smiled. 'If I can look but not touch, I shall need more coffee and a liqueur.' He raised a hand and asked for more coffee. 'Do you have this effect on every man you meet?' he asked.

'Not every one.' She smiled, and then a dreamy expression filled her eyes, making them less green and more like rain-washed lichen. One man had taken the opposite view. One man had thought her an emptyheaded girl of no importance, with no feminine attractions and very little in the way of manners. 'Some men actually find me stupid,' she said.

'Any man who thought that must be a moron,' he said. 'Just look round this room. Every male from sixteen to ninety is lusting after you whenever they can look at you without being seen to do so by their womenfolk.' He looked behind him as if to illustrate what he was saying. 'Good Grief! Talk of the Devil. Do you see who I see?'

'No,' she lied. She had seen a man staring at her and had come out of her reverie to see a pair of jasper-dark eyes looking at her as if he couldn't think where he had seen her before. 'Oh, I see who you mean,' she said, in a bored voice. 'I expect most of the medical staff come here from time to time. It might be the one place to avoid if I want to be alone.'

'Miles . . . I thought you were in Southampton.'

Miles Stratton rose from the table where he sat alone, although it was laid with two place settings. 'I came back early by plane.' He spoke to Bruce but his gaze was on Dawn.

'You two have met . . . no need to introduce you,' said Bruce Tyley, as if that disposed of formalities and they needn't make small talk. His air was slightly possessive, as if there was more to his relationship with the lovely girl than merely a dinner date for two. Amusement at his chauvinistic attitude, excluding her from further conversation, helped Dawn's sudden confusion at being confronted with Miles Stratton in a fresh and neutral meeting place.

'You're wrong, Bruce. I don't think we have met. Will you introduce me to your friend?' The dark eyes held humour and curiosity and Dawn tried to harden her heart. This man was charming, and so very good looking. She recalled the off-hand manner and the terse comments that had seared her brain on the evening when she was chilled to the bone, in pain from her pulled muscle and thoroughly miserable. She remembered the pleasure with which he goaded her into a temper, the joy he took in piling insult on insult and making her feel a fool.

'There's no need, Bruce. Dr Stratton and I have met, but evidently I made very little impression on him.' She was able to say it as if she would rather not pursue the conversation. 'I think the waiter wants to know which liqueur you want, Bruce, and I would love some more coffee.'

'I apologise,' said Miles Stratton, curtly. 'I had no wish to intrude on your *tête-à-tête*. I'll see you tomorrow, Tyley.'

'You need a Drambuie or something. You have gone quite pale. Waiter . . . more coffee, please, and two Drambuies.'

Out of the corner of her eye, Dawn saw Miles Stratton rise once more from his chair and smile at a slim, tall blonde who joined him. He settled her into her seat and resumed the chair with his back to Dawn and Bruce.

'That was sweet . . . as sweet as a nut,' crowed Bruce. 'I don't know what he did to you, Dawn, but I could feel the cold steel from here.' He gave a mock shudder. 'I can see that it doesn't do to underestimate you . . . I shall treat you with extreme caution in case I burn my hands on that fiery hair.'

'He did nothing. I just don't like him, that's all.'

'I still don't get it, but why should I worry? His loss, I hope, will be my gain.'

'Don't count on it, Bruce. I told you that I have no need or desire for more than friendship and I mean it.' She moved restlessly. The second order of coffee was a mistake. It was piping hot and there was a large silver pot of it to be finished, now that it had been ordered for her.

She dropped her table napkin and bent to pick it up, stealing a glance at the couple who seemed to be absorbed in close conversation. The blonde girl brought a thick folded paper from her large handbag and opened it while they waited for their food to arrive. Dawn glimpsed thin blue lines and shapes, as if the girl was showing Miles Stratton a plan of something. She could see no more unless she stared, and had to give Bruce her full attention for the rest of the meal.

A plan? And what had someone said . . . that he would come back to the Island after he was in the RAF using it as a base until he was married. Plans were often given to prospective house buyers. They must be thinking of buying a new house on the Isle of Wight, or the plans might be of one they were having built, a place of their own to live in when his present appointment with the local doctor lapsed and the couple could be together. It was natural, and enviable . . . two people in love making a home . . . making dreams together. The girl was laughing and her laugh was low and musical. The blonde hair was drawn back in a clasp and made the good features clear and pure. The jump-suit of coffee-coloured velvet could have looked good in an office, at home or, as now, in a restaurant, and she carried with her an indefinable chic.

She put down the paper and gathered her handbag. 'I think I left my gloves in the bar,' she said, and as she drifted past the table, Dawn smelled the expensive French perfume that trailed behind her like a cloud of sophistication. She returned, her driving gloves in her hand and smiling. Dawn looked away, but Bruce smiled and said 'Hello' as she passed.

'Who was that?' Dawn tried to sound casual.

'That's the lovely sheila that Miles goes with. I told you he pipped me with a blonde. Stephanie is just that one. A very cool lady, but sexy with it.'

'Are they married . . . engaged . . . living in?' She smiled, through dry lips. 'I might as well catch up on the gossip.'

'No . . . I can't make it out. They meet and seem to get on well and everyone thinks they have an understanding, but he doesn't bring her to the hops at the hospital or to meet any of his friends.'

'If they're like you, he might be wise to keep her to himself!'

'*Touché*. But seriously, she's a very nice person and he's wise to hang on to her.'

'They had a plan of something with them. I glimpsed it on the table. Doesn't that indicate that they might be setting up house?'

'Could be.' But he refused to discuss it further. 'Come on, we've got half an hour before closing time. I can hear strains of music and I promised you the delights of Dave Attril's accordion.'

'I don't think I like accordions.'

'Who's an ungrateful girl, then? Come on, be a sport. They'll love it if you go in and listen. Try to tap a toe now and then . . . if you can find the rhythm.'

They went through into the bar and were nearly knocked back by the fumes of the dark shag that most of the men from the boats either smoked or chewed. Dave Attril stood by the piano, carrying an enormous accordion which threatened to make him lose his balance. He was trying to play with one hand and was becoming frustrated by the dressing on his wounded hand. When he saw Dawn, he slipped the strap of the instrument from his shoulder with a sigh of relief. 'It's no use, lads, I can't play with this strapped up. Sister there will tell you I can't, won't you, Sister?'

'I think it might be rather painful if you tried tonight,' she said, and smiled. They were surrounded by a ring of curious faces and she saw Bert Cass in the corner with his cousin, drinking light ale. He raised his mug in greeting and she saw the meaning look he gave towards Bruce. Oh! she thought. This is a complication I hadn't thought of. Now, they will all think that Bruce is my boyfriend. She remembered saying that she couldn't go to the Smugglers with Bert because her boyfriend would object.

'My shout,' said Dave Attril. 'Come on,

Sister, I said I'd buy you one when you came in.'

'Can I take you up on that another time, Dave? We had wine with some food and I really shouldn't drink any more if I'm to be bright on duty tomorrow.'

He grinned. 'Can't have you being half-seas-over, Sister. Might have another little job for you to do, sometime.'

'No more fish hooks, please, Dave,' she said, and the other men laughed. One played the piano and sang old music-hall songs and a man with a shaggy beard and large sad eyes read some of his own verses that went on and on about a wreck in the old days. The applause was more for the fact that he had come to the end than for any appreciation of poetical talent, and as the land-lord called 'time gentlemen, please', they clam-oured for one more tune on the piano. Dave raised his glass. 'What's your favourite, Sister?' She shook her head, laughing. 'Well, we'll drink to you, then. To Sister Campion, who's come to look after us . . . and give us all baths . . . up at the hospital.' A roar of laughter greeted him, and Dave blushed deep pink.

'News travels at the speed of light here,' said Bruce. 'By now, the account of Mike Carter being made to take a shower has probably got to obscene proportions.' He smiled. 'But the fact remains, Dawn . . . you'll do.'

She looked towards the dining-room door and

her laughter faded. Miles Stratton was looking at her with a mixture of annoyance and amazement. He knows now that I am Sister Campion, the faceless, shapeless sister who helped him in Casualty and who refused to be drawn into polite conversation, she thought. His eyes travelled over her slim form, the high pure line of her breasts and the glory of her hair, and she turned to speak to Bruce, pretending that she had not seen him. A subtle sense of elation made her rejoice that he was the one at a disadvantage now.

'Can we get out before the rush? I'm very hot,' said Dawn. Bruce looked at the over-bright eyes and flushed face, and made a way for her to the door. The moon was a sliver of cool melon in a dark blue sky. 'That's better,' she sighed. 'The air in there was terrible.'

'Walk down to the quay,' he said. 'It's a mild night.'

'The quay? I didn't think there was one here.'

'They call it that, but it's just a jetty for fishing boats in the next small bay along. It's sheltered and not many people know about it unless they come down from the Smugglers. I think it might've been a haven for privateers in the old days.'

They walked slowly along and the sounds of night were soft and friendly.

The thin line of light, cast as a line is cast to

catch Neptune's fish, came softly from the moon across the water, and the waves had no white caps.

'Thank you for taking me there, Bruce. I wouldn't have enough self-possession to go there alone.'

'I should think not. Where I come from, women aren't encouraged to visit bars unless they are . . .'

'Unless they are tarts?'

'No . . . I didn't mean that. It just doesn't happen at home,' he said. He brightened. 'It's better here. They talk of the freedom of Australia, but I think the women here have a better deal. Take Stephanie, for example.'

'The blonde in the Smugglers?'

'Yeah. She holds down a very good job, goes everywhere a man can go and flies, too.'

'What sort of a job does she do?'

'She designs planes, would you believe? Helps do it, anyway. Works with Irene's old man and from what I hear does a first-rate job.'

Dawn smiled in the darkness. It was clear to her that Bruce had more than a passing interest in the lady, however much he seemed to deny it. A sudden thought struck her. Was she not doing a similar thing? She disliked Miles Stratton but she was becoming obsessed with wanting to know about him. With Bruce it might be a physical attraction as well as admiration for the good-looking Stephanie, but it couldn't possibly be attraction that made her thoughts turn to the handsome doctor with the sombre eyes. A tiny shiver ran down her back as, quite unbidden, the vision rose before her in the silent spaces in the rocks, of a man with soap on his shoulder and a dark mole in the creamy flesh . . .

'I'd like to go back. Irene said not to put too much weight on my leg for another day or so and I was on my feet quite a lot today on duty.'

'Can't have those lovely ankles swelling, can we?' Her heart warmed to the man at her side. He might be a bit of a rake from what she had heard, but she found him good company, and very caring.

The way back was deserted and the distant lights of the inn were dim. The cottage was outlined against the trees with the other two nestling against it. 'Who lives in the others?' Dawn asked. 'I ought to know my neigh-bours.'

'One belongs to the company that Stephanie works for and is used by personnel when they are visiting this side of the Island or if they want to work quietly on a project. It's useful and a nice place for a break. The other is let out as yours is to hospital staff who might need to be on call, so the theatre sister has that one. You'll like her, but she does tend to spend most of her off duty with a family in Ventnor, so she doesn't make many friends among the staff here.'

They paused at the gate while Dawn found her front-door key and Bruce seemed in no hurry to leave.

'Another time, you can come in for coffee, Bruce, but tonight, I am quite tired and I have to be on duty early as it's outpatients day for the medical ward.'

'I haven't far to walk,' he said. 'The house behind the hospital is very convenient for medics living out and you must see it soon.'

'Who lives there?'

'Just me and Hobart have flats there, with a room for Stratton if he wants it, but he's living down the road at the practice where he's doing the locum. A pharmacist comes and stays sometimes if the weather is bad and she's late starting back to Newport, and there are two spare rooms for visitors.'

A bat flew against the moon like a torn black glove and Dawn opened the gate. A movement from the next cottage made her turn towards Bruce and before she realised what was happening, his arms closed round her and his mouth came hard on her lips. 'No, Bruce . . . NO!' she said, and pushed him away. She saw two people at the gate of the cottage next door and even as she rushed away along the path and into the sanctuary of her temporary home, she saw the glint of blonde hair and sensed rather than saw

the stare of jasper-dark eyes watching the kiss
that the new sister had allowed the hospital
Casanova to plant on her lips.

CHAPTER FIVE

'You really have no pain?' Irene Meadows put
the huge container of unscented talcum powder
back on the shelf and slapped her hands
together, sending a small cloud-burst of powder
over her white coat.

'Only when you really put pressure on that
muscle, Irene. It's fantastic when I think back to
only two or three days ago. Yesterday I walked
up to the first rise on the Down and I'm longing to
go higher. Can I go for a really good walk along
the shore?'

'Take it easy. Walking in sand is tiring and as
for walking through shingle, it's like dragging a
ball and chain on your legs. It makes me tired!'

'I'll be careful,' said Sister Dawn Campion.
'Now what? Do I go back on duty?'

'No, your time's not up yet. Did you bring a
leotard?' Dawn nodded. 'Change quickly and
you have time for a brisk session on the cycle.'

'And you said I was to take it easy,' groaned
Dawn. She emerged from the cubicle wearing a
bright blue leotard that hugged her slim figure
and showed every line of her breasts and hips.
Irene told her to leave her shoes on the floor and

91

to cycle barefooted. The long thin line of the scar, showing where the leg had been skilfully sutured after the extensive surgical procedures that had been necessary to restore her leg into shape and ultimate working order, was dying away and the fact that she could appear without tights for her remedial sessions did much to tell Dawn that the scar was of little importance. It was wonderful to feel free, barefooted and un-restricted by tight clothes, and she began to cycle on the machine, at first slowly, and then building up her speed until the pedals flew round and her cheeks were pink with effort.

'There's no need to think you are in the run-ning for the international cycle championships,' said Irene. 'Just go as fast as is comfortable and keep it up for ten minutes. If you push the pace too much, you'll start to flag much too early . . . gently does it.'

'I see what you mean,' said Dawn, slackening her speed slightly and panting. The golden light of mid-day caught the glint of red in her hair as she sat in full sunlight. She was aware of her body as something of lightness and grace for the first time since her accident, and the set of her shoul-ders once more held the pride and confidence of youth and beauty.

'I'll have to get my hair cut,' she said. 'This kind of exercise shakes it up a bit. I must look like a fuzzy bear.' She heard the sound of a heavy box being put down on the table and thought that she was calling to Irene, but when there was no reply she glanced back to see who had come in behind her.

'I wouldn't say that,' said a cool, deep voice. She tried to turn back even more and felt herself slipping from the narrow, shiny saddle of the machine. Desperately, she clung to the handle bars, but her body had slipped too far and her balance had gone.

'Here, let me help you . . .' The voice was amused, but Dawn Campion could see nothing funny in being humiliated once more in front of Dr Miles Stratton. His strong arms lifted her bodily from the machine before she fell any further, and her hold was torn from the handle bars. 'Let go . . . if you fall, you must learn to let go,' he said, calmly. 'How can we expect you to do parachute training if you can't even fall from a bicycle in the correct manner?'

'Parachute training? What on earth do you mean? In any case, it was all your fault,' she stormed. 'Do you make a habit of creeping up on people and frightening them out of their wits?'

'Most people don't scare that easily. You knew that Irene was in here, so it should have been no surprise to hear someone moving about. What's in that to scare you?' He grinned, and Dawn suddenly realised that he still held her close, with her feet resting on his shining brown shoes. She was furious, but behind her anger she recognised the absurdity of the situation. She had the minimum of clothes on and was standing barefooted on his feet as if she were a child being taken for a walk like this, or pretending to dance with a grown-up. The only difference was the sensation she had of his nearness, the sensuous delight she experienced from the hardness of his hand on her back and the other round her shoulders. This was no pretend dance with a favourite uncle, but the heady contact of a female form with a male whose body was taut and strong and awakened in her feelings of which she had never dreamed . . .

'Put me down,' she said, softly, and glanced up at him. She saw the muscles of his face tighten and the dark eyes showed no expression. 'Thank you,' she said, as he deposited her on a chair. She was increasingly aware of the fact that she had worn no bra under the tight leotard, but had revelled in the uncluttered freedom, but now, the scoop neckline of the stretch material showed the gentle dip to the full cleavage only seen in such clothes. She hitched the shoulder up on one side, but it only made the dip more revealing and she couldn't control her uneven breathing.

'How many kilometres have you done?' He looked at the gauge. 'And what is more interesting, why?'

'Irene,' she called. 'May I go now?' Irene put

her head round the door and nodded. 'I'll see you tomorrow,' said Dawn.

'Finished? I rather hoped that we could have had a fall or two on the mat . . . karate, of course,' said Dr Stratton with a grin. 'What is this? Keep fit for the nursing staff? I thought that this was a busy department.'

'If you mean that am I wasting hospital time and facilities, the answer is no.'

'I was bound to wonder,' he said. 'I come in here in time to see one very healthy and blooming casualty sister working away at the apparatus with all the energy of a dedicated athlete in training. Or are you limbering up to tackle Mike Carter when he comes back for treatment?'

'I can handle Mike without training,' she said, shortly.

'I think you can handle most men . . . when you want to do so,' he said, enigmatically.

She blushed, recalling the two people who had witnessed the fervour of Bruce Tyley's goodnight kiss. So, Dr Stratton had seen them. He had not been too busy saying goodnight to the blonde and attractive Stephanie who had claimed all his attention in the restaurant of the Smugglers Rest.

'I don't have much to do with men unless they are patients,' she said. She blushed. That was asking for the lifted eyebrow, and the sardonic glance he gave her. It was better to keep quiet before she made more *faux pas*.

'Dawn . . . are you still there?' Irene came back, drying her hands. 'Sorry I had to leave you, but I have another patient in there who was getting near the end of his heat treatment, so I massaged his back and left him to dress. Put some oil or baby cream on the scar before you dress.'

Dr Miles Stratton glanced at her legs. 'You really have come here for treatment,' he said.

'Of course she has, Miles.' Irene sounded irritated. 'What do you think I'm doing? Setting up a yoga class for the nursing staff?' She bustled away, muttering that she was busy even if he wasn't.

Dawn took the bottle of baby lotion and walked past the man who watched every movement she made. She went into the cubicle to change and felt more confident when her legs were covered and she was fully dressed. Irene was talking to the doctor and Dawn wondered if she could slip away without further conversation with the disturbing and annoying man, but Irene called her back from the door.

'Look at this, Dawn. I'm sure that Miles would like your opinion of this box.'

She looked at the black box that Dr Miles Stratton had set on the table. 'What is it?' she asked.

'It's a dummy run of a first-aid box for the staff

using the ambulance flights. Pick it up,' he ordered.

'Why? Is it going to explode?' She laughed to hide her true feelings. To be standing close to the man whose touch disturbed her, made her cheeks glow—laughter was the only weapon to use against the growing physical attraction she felt for him.

'I want to know if the average nursing sister could carry it for a distance of say . . . a hundred yards in an emergency. If we pack too much into it, we shall defeat our own objective of being quickly on the scene with instant aid.' She lifted it fairly easily. 'Good . . . now walk across the room with it as if you were in a hurry.'

Dawn gripped the box by its leather handle, after passing the shoulder strap over her shoulder to take most of the strain, and did as he said. As she walked away, with the heavy weight on her shoulder, she knew that she limped slightly . . . not as much as she had done the night she nearly lost her luggage over the side of the ferry, but enough to remind her of the occasion, and enough to show Dr Stratton that this member of the staff of the St Boniface Cottage Hospital walked with a limp, even though she bore no resemblance to the silly girl he had met when she was wearing the ridiculous yellow knitted hat that covered every strand of the beautiful auburn hair.

She turned back, avoiding his gaze. She looked at Irene, who smiled and made matters far worse. 'You walk beautifully now, Dawn. I can hardly believe that you had such weakness in that leg when you first came here.' She laughed. 'I take a little of the credit for that, but you have worked hard to get back full function.'

'Yes,' said Dr Miles Stratton, with a slow grin. 'There's nothing wrong with your legs, Sister.'

'And that's another thing,' said Irene, happily oblivious to any tension. 'She was hiding behind thick black tights, thinking it hid the scar, but I told her she'd feel much better and look good in sheer tights again.'

'I *had* noticed,' he said, solemnly. Dawn put the box back on the table. 'In a hurry to get away, Sister?' His voice was smooth and, she thought, mocking.

'I've finished my treatment and have to check one or two things before I go off duty,' she said, stiffly. 'So, if you don't need me for any more . . . research, I'd like to go back and do something more constructive than parade my legs.'

His face darkened and she almost wished she had sounded less rude. I wasn't as rude as he was to me, she thought, defensively, but it gave her no comfort.

'I would like two more minutes of your time, Sister,' he said. 'I'm sure that even you will think this useful. Please look inside and tell me in what order the contents should be packed.'

She opened the box and took out a thick wad of gamgee tissue wrapped in plastic film. She fingered the thick pack of cotton wool enclosed on both sides by fine gauze which was used to pad wounds or to soak up blood or discharge, to be used as incontinence pads or, in an emergency, even to pad splints. The next layer was a mixture of dressings and under them was a pack of sterile instruments, a pack of sterile gloves and bottles of lotions, phials of drugs and sterile plastic syringes.

'A tray would be useful,' Dawn said, interested in spite of her haste to get away from Miles Stratton. She took out all the contents and set them out on the table. 'If there was a tray with raised edges, it would be cleaner than the ground near the accident. Assuming that someone was found on a cliff ledge with blood flowing from a wound, you would need swabs and lotions first, unless he was so bad that all you could do was to pad the wound and hope to get him to hospital before much harm was done.' She stood and looked at the collection of first-aid equipment.

'Well, what do you think? The tray is a good idea. It would supply a level surface on which to set out syringes or instruments or dressings.' The quiet voice was no longer mocking.

'A tray could slot down the side so that it could be used or left out of the way if it wasn't needed.

Two compartments for drugs and lotions, and dry dressings in the other in case of accidents to the box . . . the things you need first at the top and the padding at the bottom, with perhaps one pad to protect the top of the contents and to be used to make pressure on a bleeding point . . . to pad a splint or just to mop up.' She glanced at the serious face above her. 'What about vacuum flasks of coffee? An extra exposure blanket of some insulating material like they use for mountain rescue? They come in quite small packs and are very good, I believe. My cousin helps in rescues in some of the holes in Mendip and the blankets are not bulky and preserve body heat.'

'Preventing hypothermia?'

She looked up and his eyes held a secret smile.

'Yes,' she said. 'Very important.' To her annoyance, her colour was rising again and she sensed his amusement.

'And do you get air-sick, Sister?' he asked.

'No . . . but that isn't important, Dr Stratton. Ask the person who will be using this equipment. I shall not be with you.'

'I think you will,' he said, firmly. 'I'll even let you wear that awful yellow hat. It would pinpoint you on the cliff and lead us to you!'

'No way,' she said. 'I doubt if we could work together for long, Dr Stratton. Each time we have met, you have managed to be rude to me in some way. We have to meet if and when you bring patients here, but apart from my work here, I think you would still consider me to be . . . what was it? A numbskull?' She put the large pad of gamgee tissue on the table and smiled, bleakly. 'I must go back to my work,' she said, and walked out, her head held high, the warm blood in her cheeks, and her breast heaving with indignation.

As she left, she heard Irene's irritated voice. 'What on earth are you doing, Miles? Don't you know a really good nurse when you meet one? No wonder the poor girl dislikes you.'

So it wasn't just her own opinion. Irene was ready to admit that the wonderful Dr Miles Stratton was less than polite on occasion. She remembered the way he held her when she slipped from the cycling machine and wished that her stupid heart would settle down to its regular beat. Why couldn't I react to someone like Bruce in this way, she thought, but amended that wish when she recalled that he was perhaps more dangerous . . . the hospital Lothario.

Think of the Devil! 'Hello, Bruce,' she said. 'What brought you here?'

'Just passing and wondered if you would like to walk a little this afternoon. I believe that you are off duty?' She nodded. 'You'll come?' His cautious smile became boyish and eager. 'You've forgiven me?'

'I think so,' she said, severely. 'Just watch it

and make sure it doesn't happen again, Bruce.'
She smiled, making her lips curl up at the corners. 'It's a lovely day and I do want to go for a
walk.'

'It's not as warm as it looks. For April, the air
is mild, but when the breeze springs up, it can be
nippy. I should bring a hat or a scarf to wear on
your head, then we needn't turn back unless a
storm comes.' He looked at the clock in Casualty. 'Meet you in half an hour?'

'I'll be at the cottage,' she said. 'But better
make it three quarters of an hour. I haven't eaten
lunch yet.'

'What have you been doing?'

'Irene gives me physiotherapy and I cycled
about a hundred miles on that terrible treadmill.'

'Worth every rev: you've lost your limp completely.'

'Yes, my leg is back to normal,' she said. As
she walked into the dining room, she wondered
why her reactions were so different to the very
similar appraisals of the two doctors. Bruce
viewed her legs with frank admiration and
almost amusing lechery, and she could laugh
about it, but Miles Stratton made her feel uncomfortable, as if his emotions were not the
same under the smooth surface. Were his
thoughts darker . . . more sinister? Yet she
couldn't in all fairness believe that, after seeing
the gentle care he lavished on his patients.

'Have you seen the notice board?' said one of the other sisters, shrugging. 'Not for me . . . I'm medical and I hate heights. It calls for volunteers, but I can think of only you and Theatre Sister who would qualify for it. Rather you than me,' she added as she carried her curried lamb to the table.

Dawn slipped out to look at the notice board in the main hall. It held a large notice asking for volunteers for the new emergency service. Anyone who thought they could be useful was asked to sign and to give details of off duty for the next two weeks.

'That's not fair,' said Dawn.

'What's not fair?' said Irene who came up behind her.

'It says anyone who thinks they can be useful, not anyone who wishes to volunteer. It takes away the choice of anyone who is used to working with emergencies of a surgical nature.'

'Well, it doesn't follow that all volunteers are suitable. You can't substitute enthusiasm for real skill. This isn't a romantic idea of helping handsome ship-wrecked sailors by putting a white bandage on the fevered brow! This calls for nerve and skill and the kind of personality that goes with acute surgical care,' said Irene.

'Well, they'll be lucky if they find anyone to come up to their high standards,' said Dawn, crisply. 'Coming to eat?'

'You haven't signed.'

'I don't *have* to sign anything,' said Dawn, stubbornly. 'If cases come here, I don't mind getting up at night if it's necessary, but I can't think they need me when there are lots of others from the hospitals in Newport and Ryde who might like to pant after Dr Stratton and his ilk, to do his bidding and be patted on the head for it.'

'I'd like to slap you when you talk like that,' Irene said. 'Can't you get it into your head that this is not an arena to fight out personal hates? This is something that might help save lives. If it saved only one life, it would be worth it. Think about it. There's no immediate rush as the stretchers haven't yet arrived. They are special ones that can slot along the sides of the plane interior. My old man is bringing them here tonight, ready for fixing.' She moved to the side board and sniffed. 'Lamb curry or salad and ham. I'll take the curry, it's not as warm as the sun would have us believe.'

'That's what Bruce said . . . I think I'll put on warm cords this afternoon,' said Dawn.

'Going out with him again?'

'I've been out with him once . . . another demure walk added to one dinner doesn't mean I spend all my time with him,' said Dawn. She slapped her plate down on the table as if she was also swatting a fly. 'At least he treats me as a woman likes to be treated . . . he's never rude or sarcastic.'

Irene shrugged. 'Take care he doesn't treat you as he does some of his amours. No . . . don't look so cross. He has a bad name, Dawn, and I wouldn't touch him with a ten-foot pole if I were you.' She smiled. 'I admit he's good looking and great fun at a party, but just be careful.'

'I think I can handle him,' said Dawn. 'I think you're a little hard on him.'

'We all are at times with someone or other,' said Irene with a meaning glance.

'If you mean Dr Stratton, let's not talk about him, shall we?'

'I'm an interfering bitch. Tell you what, my old man will be here tonight. We'll call for you after duty and take you for a drink. I want you to meet him, and he has heard a lot about you already.'

'That will be nice. I shall look forward to it. Do you mind if I go now? I said I'd meet Bruce in fifteen minutes from now.'

She almost ran back to the cottage and rummaged for her emerald-green cord trousers, the soft mohair sweater of rusty gold that almost hid her in its folds and generous collar, which she wore over a tight-fitting long-sleeved cotton tee-shirt for extra warmth. She thrust the yellow knitted hat deep into the back of her wardrobe and perched a green beret topped with a bobble on her bright hair. With a padded raincoat of cinnamon cotton over her arm, she walked down the stairs, pleased that her leather Western boots no longer pressed on swollen muscles, but sat snugly and warmly on her calves.

There was no need to ask if she looked good. Bruce stood and stared, his mouth puckering into a slow whistle, and he insisted on adding her coat to the one he had slung over his arm. 'I can't offer to carry your handbag,' he said, with a grin. 'I'm not the type . . . and you make me feel very . . . masculine.'

'What you need is a good long walk to use up your energy,' she said, but she couldn't be annoyed with him.

The short turf of the slope up to Tennyson Down was soft and springy, with the early promise of long rye grass at the edges where the cliff top loomed over the sea. This was the place of rabbits and harebells, she remembered from childhood, and she put back her head to breathe in deeply and let the sun blaze into her closed eyelids as she paused for breath half way to the top. A wooden seat offered them rest, but Bruce dragged her away, promising that the view was even better the higher they went, and, laughing, they half ran, half climbed until the water on either side of the hill showed blue, making them rulers of a tiny peninsula high above the world.

The breeze tore at her hat and she rescued it and thrust it into the pocket of her coat. Her hair flew out and her scalp tingled, tugged by the breeze seraphs.

'You look wonderful,' Bruce said.

'I feel it. I haven't felt so free for months . . . years. I love this place. I always knew that I'd come back, but I never dreamed that I'd work here.'

They walked on and stared fascinated down into deep rocky gullies that cleft the side of the hill and let in the angry waves. Gulls swooped and cried their desolation to the empty, wide sky below the tufted clouds and the bright sun. The wind was cold up on the Down and there was no place to shelter, and Dawn insisted that she had done enough for one day and must go back on duty for the evening.

'I am off now so that Nurse Brody can be off tonight,' she said. 'I expect she would like to catch an early bus into Newport where she stays for some of her time off.'

'Not tonight . . . she's staying locally.'

'How do you know? Is she your date for tonight?' Dawn teased.

'You haven't seen the list?'

'What list?'

'I thought you couldn't have seen it as you haven't signed. Nurse Brody signed and I remember her off duty was marked with a tick meaning that she would be available for an emergency.'

Dawn was silent and pretended that all her attention was needed for finding a way through some brambles.

'It might be fun,' he went on. 'Not that I want to be left all night on a draughty ledge with Nurse Brody . . . or even with that nice little thing you have with you as an assistant.' He moved closer. 'But you and I would make a good team, Dawn, on or off duty.'

She moved away and gave him a warning smile. 'I must get back, Bruce. I said she could go early today. I also think I've walked far enough and I'm dying for a cup of tea.'

'My place or yours?' he said.

'Neither. I really am going back early and having tea in my office.' She relented. 'You can wander along if you like and have a sticky bun.'

He handed her into his dusty car and she found that it was good to rest her leg again. 'This car may be old, but there are times when I couldn't be without it,' he said. 'Your leg aching?'

'A little, but nothing like it did last week. Every time I give it exercise, it is that much better, but I agree about the car . . . it's a marvellous luxury after a brisk walk. When I came here last, I had to take the bus, and you know how few there are out of season.'

'Not far as the crow flies, but too much for you

yet.' He glanced sideways at her blooming cheeks. 'I'll have to look after you if you are to come surfing with me,' he said.

'It's much too cold! I don't think I could put a toe in until June,' she said.

'I don't mean here . . . I mean at home in Australia.'

'That might be warmer,' she said.

'Much warmer. You will come, Dawn?'

'If I'm passing,' she said, casually.

'I've been very good this afternoon,' he said. 'I've wanted to kiss you at least a hundred times. When you come home with me, you won't be passing on, Dawn . . . try to get used to the idea.' He stopped the car and ran round to open the door for her. His hand was warm on her wrist as he helped her from the car. 'Remember that I don't give up easily, and now I shall come back for sticky buns and tea in half an hour.'

She watched him go and the sensation he left in her heart was one of sadness. He left no lingering frisson of contact behind, no emotion other than that generated by a loving friend. It should be enough, she told herself. It should be more than enough to accept the love of a good-looking man who admired her so blatantly, but she knew that her love, when it bloomed, would burst like the petals of a rare and precious flower, fragrant and passionate, when a touch from her beloved would sear into her heart with pain and longing.

She walked past the notice board on her way on duty and hesitated, nearly adding her name to the three signatures already there, but she tightened her lips. Miles Stratton would never take her seriously if she had to work with him, and she . . . would take his nearness much too seriously, and lack concentration when it came to a serious emergency. If I think he's laughing at me or being sarcastic, I can't hope to do my job properly, she thought, unhappily. But as Bruce had said, it would be fun . . . and so much more.

She made tea and poured a cup for Nurse Brody who now seemed in no hurry to go.

'It was lovely up there on Tennyson Down,' Dawn said.

'Might be blowing a gale by morning,' said Nurse Brody. 'Mike Carter came in to have his dressing changed and he said he had put his boat on the beach for a day or two.'

'I thought he would be trawling tonight.'

'No, he had a good catch last night and they stayed on crabbing until mid-day, checking their pots in case they worked free in a storm.'

'He seems very sure. It's a lovely day and even the sky isn't all that stormy. A bit of herringbone high up over the Solent, but nothing bad.' She opened the bag of fresh buns she had bought on the way back. 'But I'd be the last to tell Mike his business. They've lived and worked here long enough to know what they're talking about.'

'May I come in?' said a solemn voice. 'I heard that there were buns for tea.' Nurse Brody looked annoyed. 'Have no fear, Nurse Brody. I *am* invited today. In fact, I brought some chocolate biscuits to add to the feast.'

'You could come more often if you brought these with you,' said Brody, putting the biscuits on a dish and helping herself to two of them.

'What it is to be popular,' he sighed. 'Now I know the path to your heart, Nurse.' He grinned at Dawn. 'I wonder what the path is to yours, Sister?'

She laughed. 'Harebells from the undercliff . . . lad's death and other rare plants from dangerous places,' she said, 'and if you die getting them, I'll never speak to you again.' They laughed, but Dawn wished she had kept quiet. Even as a joke, she had no right to laugh at the risks that could be met on those green clifftops.

'I'd rather dive for buried treasure or abalone shells, but you'd have to come and watch me,' he said.

'There aren't any shells like that in England,' said Nurse Brody.

'Exactly,' he said, calmly, helping himself to his third bun and licking the sticky sugar from his fingers with satisfaction.

'You can give me any report now, Nurse,' Dawn said. 'You've made up the notes about dressings?'

'Yes, Sister. I took out the drain in Mike Carter's incision and it's clean and healing well from the base. Dave Attril looked in to say that the dressing was off and he didn't need another. It looked all right, Sister. I felt around it for fluctuation and heat, but it was quite cool and painless. There are just two dark marks where the hook went in and came out again, but he's delighted.' She gave details of two other dressings and gathered up her notes. 'May I go, now?'

'Of course. Are you going away? It's your day off tomorrow, and I know you have friends on the Island.'

'I shall go into Newport tomorrow, but I have a friend coming over this evening for a meal in the Smugglers.' She turned to Bruce Tyley, a note of pride in her voice. 'I'm on call as from today if there is an emergency on this side of the Island.'

'So I saw,' said Bruce. 'Have you added your valuable signature, Sister?'

'I . . . that is, I can't do that until I have the Okay about my leg,' Dawn said, weakly. 'I would be a liability if I went out and my leg gave out, wouldn't I?'

'Your accident must have made you a bit nervous,' said Brody with understanding. 'I think you're wise to give it a week or so.' She grinned. 'I don't mind. I hope I get something exciting to do. I can't tell you how I'm looking forward to it, aren't you, Dr Tyley?'

'Thrilling,' he said, but he was looking at Dawn with a puzzled expression. 'I'm sure that when the time comes, anyone who can take out a fish hook as Sister did, will never flinch from doing what she has to do.'

'I suppose I could help in some capacity,' she said. It was becoming embarrassing. At first she had thought that it would be a casual arrangement, with few people knowing about it and no mention of it appearing on the hospital notice board. 'I could pack the first-aid boxes,' she added, weakly.' Bruce laughed. 'Well, someone has to do them,' she said.

'Anyone can do that, but you have special talents. You're not air sick, are you?'

'No,' she said. 'I'm fine in boats and in the air. I just don't think I'd be much use.'

'What rubbish. The sooner you get your name down, the better.' He grinned. 'It will give me time to make sure I'm on the same shift as you.'

'All right, if you promise not to let me fall over the edge of the cliff,' she said, lightly. She took a deep breath. 'I'll do it now before I chicken out.' It was better to let them think she felt inadequate for the work than to show that she was afraid of being with Dr Miles Stratton for any longer than was absolutely necessary.

The telephone rang and when she had

answered it and cleared away the tea tray because Nurse Peebles had yet to come back from
the ward where she had been working as relief
during the tea break, she switched on the light in
her office. It was getting dark and it was later
than she had thought. Bruce had gone to make a
ward round and the corridors were silent. I can't
face him or Nurse Brody again if I haven't added
my name to the list, she thought. Nurse Peebles
came back and her last excuse vanished. 'I shall
be gone for ten minutes at the longest, Nurse,'
she said. 'I have to go down to the main hall.'

'Yes, Sister. I'll take any messages and tell
them you'll be back.'

The window in the lower corridor faced west
and was banging open on a badly fitting latch.
Dawn stopped to fix it and found that the wind
was becoming very strong. She listened and
heard the trees sighing against the gusts. In the
main hall, she studied the list and added her
name with the times of her off duty for the next
few days. She ticked the times when she would
be in the neighbourhood of the hospital, in-
cluding that evening. They can get me at the
Smugglers, she thought.

On the way back to the department, at the
back of the building, the wind didn't sound as
strong and she dismissed it from her mind, until
the telephone rang.

CHAPTER SIX

'Did you come along by the jetty?' Dawn asked anxiously, as the night sister came to check that the department was empty of patients and whether the nurse detailed to look after it during the night was busy packing drums, or would be available to help elsewhere in the cottage hospital if required.

'No, I came straight from the bus and changed here at the cottage where Theatre Sister lives.' She looked at the new sister's anxious face, and beyond her to a trolley which was laid up with sterile towels and bowls, ready for the addition of instruments if they were required. 'What's up?'

'Nothing so far, but Mike Carter rang earlier asking if Dr Miles Stratton was here. He saw a small boat out in the bay with one sail trailing in the water and wondered if Dr Stratton had heard of anyone in trouble.'

'And had he?'

'He's not here, but Dr Tyley went down to the jetty with Mike to see if there was anything they could do.' She shuddered. 'That was hours ago. I've been trying to get hold of the coastguard station, but the line is bad or down completely. Listen to that wind.'

The howling of a hundred hungry wolves seemed to surround the small hospital and the solid walls threw back the sound as if shaking off an invasion.

'I'm off duty now, but I shall be in the Smugglers or in the cottage if I'm needed,' she said. All reservations about her abilities to deal with accidents, and Dr Miles Stratton, had vanished. The value of her long training at the Princess Beatrice Hospital in London took over and Dawn Campion was in no doubt that she must be available to help in any way possible, should an emergency arise. The telephone call, with Mike shouting as if he wasn't used to using the instrument, had made her realise just how close to danger were any who lived by the sea or sailed on the sea.

'Have you contacted Dr Stratton?' asked Night Sister.

'No. I don't know where he is. He was here this morning and Irene Meadows said that he was going to meet her husband to bring him here this evening, but he hasn't been seen yet.'

'Francis Meadows has a private plane, hasn't he?'

'He has one of his own, a four-seater, and a slightly larger one that he's fitting out for the new ambulance service, but surely they can't fly in this weather?' Dawn's heart was playing tricks. She would be sorry to hear of anyone being involved in an accident, but she found that she was specially anxious about Dr Stratton, the man who was all that she hated and loved. 'Matron asked me to use this phone if I tried to contact the coastguard, so that the other outside telephone will be free for local hospital calls. I'll try once more before I go off duty, and if I can't raise them, I'll go down to the beach and tell Mike and Dr Tyley, if they're still there.'

She dialled the number and heard a rasping sound. 'That's more than I heard earlier. The telephone is working, over some lines, so the fault must be their end.' She tried once more and a dim voice answered her. Excitedly, she shouted to the man on the other end of the line that there was a boat in distress in the bay. More crackling and the line cleared. 'Did you hear me?' she called.

'The line has been down here, Miss. Would you repeat that?'

She told him that Mike Carter and Dr Tyley were at the small jetty trying to see what was happening to the small boat.

'Could someone go and see if they are still there? The situation may have resolved itself and we may need our men for other boats,' he said, calmly, with the authority of one who has seen it happen many times and refuses to be flustered.

'I'll go. I'll ring back in half an hour,' said Dawn.

She rushed over to the cottage to change and was nearly bowled over by the wind. Clutching her duty cap with one hand, she unlocked the door of the cottage, her cloak billowing round her and nearly blinding her as the breeze played with it. Warm clothes . . . that was it. Very warm clothes if she was to be out for a long time. She put the kettle to boil and changed, quickly, listening for the whistling kettle to tell her it was time to fill the two large flasks she had rinsed out and into which she now put coffee. She slung a holdall across her shoulders containing the flasks and the rest of the buns, some chocolate and biscuits.

The way to the jetty was dark and she was glad to have her powerful torch with her again. The light danced before her, allowing her to walk quickly and safely and she heard a man's voice calling.

'Can't be Dave . . . he's on stand-by for the life-boat,' said Mike Carter.

'It's me . . . Dawn Campion,' shouted Dawn against the wind. Breathlessly, she sank down on to a rock at the edge of the water. 'The . . . coastguard wants to know . . .' she panted. 'He wants to know . . . and I said I'd ring back. The line was down for ages, but they've fixed it now.'

Bruce Tyley rubbed his numbed hands

together. 'They're still out there, but the tide is coming in, so they can't get swept away. We waited for the tide to turn and now I think the boat at least will drift in on the rocks . . . but God knows what's happened to the poor blighters aboard.'

'Have you seen any sign of life?'

'Not a thing. Either the skipper is down below, probably hurt, or he's lost.' He shivered. 'It's bloody cold.'

'Here.' Dawn poured some of the hot coffee into the cup and handed it to him. She did the same for Mike who growled his thanks like a pleased bear. She rummaged for the buns and the two men ate them all. At least I can give a little warmth and food, she thought. 'What shall I do? I said I'd ring back,' she asked them.

'Tell them we'll wait until the boat is fast on the rocks, and then Mike says it will be safe enough to go out in his motorboat and climb the rest of the way along to the spit.' He grinned. 'They will be glad to leave it with us. Mike here has been in this situation himself, so he knows all about it, from both sides of the scene. Right, Mike?'

'Right.' Mike moved his shoulder as if it hurt.

'Are you all right? The cold will make your shoulder stiff. Have you enough warm clothes with you?'

'I'm fine, Sister.' He grinned in the torchlight.

'I haven't been warm since you made me have that durned bath. Took all my natural oil out of my skin.'

'Get along with you. Anyone would think you were a sheep!' she said. 'Give me the flasks and I'll bring some more when I've rung the coast-guard.'

A shadow on the water became a life-belt, driven in on the advancing tide. 'Tide's coming fast. We could get out there soon, Doctor,' said Mike. 'How's your boots? Need heavy ribs on the bottoms for this or you'll be on your arse in five seconds.'

'My boots are fine, but I could do with a thick sweater. Can you drive, Dawn?'

'I could drive your car,' she said. 'It's the same model that I hired last year on holiday.'

'Good. Can you go to my room and get the blue fisherman's sweater from the top drawer, some thick socks and an old duffle you'll find behind the door?' He grinned. 'Not all for me, but there might be someone out there who'll need it. Bring them and a bottle of brandy from the cupboard and my black bag is already in the car. Check it for coramine and morphine.' His voice was crisp and impersonal and she reacted with speed and pleasure in knowing exactly what to do.

'Sister . . .'

'Yes, Mike?'

'Got any more buns?'

She laughed and promised to find what she could and hitched her holdall high across her shoulders. Her hair was tangled in the wind and the cheeky little beret was no match for the weather. She thrust the useless hat into her pocket and tried to keep the hair from her eyes, climbing carefully back to the road.

The coastguard asked if Mike had any flares and when Dawn told them that he had, they said they would leave it to the people on the scene to cope unless something urgent turned up. It all sounded so casual, but Dawn knew that behind the slow unconcern was the expertise and dedication of generations of men who had faced storms and high water, death and maiming to rescue others needing their assistance. She felt very humble as she put the telephone back in its rest. None of these men, except for a few from the local manor house and sailing venues, could have received any education beyond the normal school instruction, but when faced with these situations, they could cope with common sense and intelligence beyond the scope of most university graduates.

She found the right key on the heavy key ring that Bruce threw to her on the beach and unlocked his bedroom door. She quickly found the clothes and the brandy and looked round the room for the duffle coat which didn't seem to be where Bruce had left it. She went into the small kitchen and decided that it would save time if she made the fresh coffee there as she could see a large jar of a famous brand of instant coffee on the table. She put water to boil and fetched the bag from Bruce's car. I can check it all here and drive straight back to the jetty, she thought. She found a large but rather stale cake in a tin and laughed softly. Bruce had a reputation for meanness when it came to bringing his share of cake when coffee or tea was served in the various departments of the hospital. He would come in, looking hopeful, accept the tea, having gauged to a minute when he thought it would be ready, then dive into the cake tin or take the best of the biscuits before the busy sister or her staff had the time to sit down.

'This time, it's your turn, Bruce,' she said. She put the cake, cut into slices ready for eating, into a plastic bag and added it to her pile of things to take. The duffle coat was behind the door of the kitchen and she reached up to take it from the rather high hook. She half closed the door to reach the coat and as she reached up, the door met a resistance as someone pushed from the other side. Another impatient push sent her spinning away from the door, still clutching the thick material. Half squashed, she tried to push back. 'Who is it? Stop messing about, Bruce. I'm trapped.'

The door was jerked forward, with the young casualty sister still clinging on for support. A head came round the door and the tall dark man with smouldering eyes slid into the kitchen.

'What are you doing here, hiding behind kitchen doors?'

'I wasn't hiding . . . I thought you were Bruce.'

'Spare me the details . . . If you *must* play peekaboo with your men friends, don't mind me.' His face was tense and pale and angry.

'I was collecting some clothes for Bruce, Dr Stratton,' Dawn said, coldly. 'He said he was getting cold.' She stepped past him to the working top of the sink and turned off the kettle.

'Hardly the weather for picnics,' he said, sarcastically.

'This is no picnic, Dr Stratton.' She filled the two flasks and put sugar in a twist of paper to take with them. She opened a high cupboard and found some coffee whitener which she took down.

'While you are doing that, may I have some?' She glanced back, an angry retort on her lips, annoyed that he should demand her attention when she was hurrying to get back to two cold hungry men and possibly someone injured or suffering from exposure. He was sitting on a kitchen chair and his face was very pale.

'Of course,' she said. 'You look terrible. Are

you starting the flu?' She poured coffee for him and, without asking, added a slug of brandy before handing it to him.

'Thanks.' He sipped it gratefully. 'I'm sorry if I frightened you,' he said. The apology was formal and there was more that was left unsaid. 'This is very good.'

'I have to go. I promised Bruce that I wouldn't be long.'

He looked at the bundle of clothes and the pack of food and drink. 'I take it that he's moving in with you.' The voice was flat and it was impossible to tell if there was resignation or condemnation in his tone.

'You have never thought very highly of me, Dr Stratton, and I have no doubt that whatever I did would be wrong in your eyes, but I can assure you, even if it is none of your business, that Bruce is not moving in with me. I am taking these things down to the jetty to prevent two men from freezing. Mike Carter and Bruce have been down there for hours, waiting to help a small boat in trouble.'

He stared, then shook his head as if to free it from a cloud, then took another gulp of coffee. His colour was returning fast and although he looked very tired, his eyes held their usual jasper-brightness. 'What do you mean?' he demanded.

'If you'd been here when they were looking for

you, you would have heard. There's a yacht out there heading for the rocks, if it isn't already fast, and Mike is going as far out along the spit as soon as possible in his motor boat.'

'He's mad. He can't get out as far as the end of the rocks in that, without going fast on the rocks himself.'

'He says he can climb the rocks and crawl along the line of the submerged ridge when the tide leaves it half exposed.' She poured some more coffee for him. 'You should get to bed,' she said. 'I'm sure you have a virus infection.'

'I'm just tired.' He gave her a glance of unveiled displeasure. 'I haven't been idle. Francis Meadows asked me to help him fit out the plane and we tried it out at Sandown.'

'What happened?' Suddenly, she knew that she had misjudged him.

'The wind was too high . . . but that was the whole idea, to see how it reacted in a storm. We have to know the dangers and the possibilities that it can offer.'

'So you deliberately took it up in this storm?'

'Someone had to do it. It's a sturdy old craft and we managed very well. We could do with a helicopter, but it will be useful.' He yawned. 'It took us the best part of the day and then the engine failed and we had to hoof it for miles to get a tractor before the tide came up and made it impossible to get it off the sands.'

'I'm sorry,' she said, almost in a whisper.

'How sorry? As sorry as I am for jumping to conclusions . . . that is, if I *was* wrong?' His dark glance sought her troubled gaze and he stood before her, his dark hair as untidy as her own blown tresses. He touched her shoulders and bent to kiss her, gently. 'Funny little thing, aren't you?' He gave a tired grin. 'You should be wearing that awful hat . . . do you know that more body heat is lost from the top of the head than from any other part of the body? Here.' From his pocket, he took a folded sailing cap which he pulled down over her hair. 'Very fetching,' he said. 'Don't lose it.'

She turned away and ran from the cottage, hoping that he would think she was anxious to get back to the others. How could she stay when the touch of his hands and the quiet kiss made her heart ache so terribly? How was she to stay now that she wore his cap . . . his grubby, creased and totally wonderful cap that smelled of masculine shampoo and the indefinable something that made it his? And he still isn't convinced that there is nothing between me and Bruce, she thought, resentfully.

She was greeted with enthusiasm as she stopped the car as close to the beach as was safe now that the tide was rising fast. Bruce laughed when he saw the cake. 'I can take a season ticket for refreshments now when I come to Cas. That is a very big cake.'

'And stale, too. Where did you get it?' she said.

'A present from Stephanie, if you must know.'

'I beg your pardon.' She laughed. 'If I had known it was a keepsake from a lovely blonde, I would never have opened the tin and taken it.'

'She said it would keep for weeks,' he said, chewing the dry cake.

'Did she say how many weeks? This must have been sitting there for *months*.'

'I suppose it was months since we . . . it's fairly old,' he said.

Mike had no such reservations but munched happily. He had dragged his small boat to the edge of the water and was waiting for the swell to die down. The wind gusted, but was not as strong and he said it would blow itself out by the morning.

'The seas will still be high,' said Bruce. 'That's when we might be able to help. If it's very rough, more harm would be done taking the patient by boat than would be the case if we left him here.'

'I think the plane has a hitch,' said Dawn and told them that she had seen Miles Stratton.

'Was Stephanie with him?' Bruce's voice was sharp.

'No, but he looked very tired. He's been with

Francis Meadows all day. He didn't mention Stephanie.'

A cloud parted long enough for the quarter moon to point out the boat that was scraping against the rocks with a sickening lurch every time the waves took it in closer. 'We'd best get on,' said Mike, laconically. 'Give us a drop of that brandy, Sister, in my flask.' She poured the golden liquid into a grime-encrusted pocket flask and hoped that the inside was cleaner or that the spirit was strong enough to be self-sterilising! Mike held the boat as steady as he could while Bruce jumped into the bow, then pushed off and jumped in with surprising agility for such a thick-set man. 'We'll take a look,' he said.

'What if there's nobody on board?' shouted Dawn.

Mike grinned, showing white teeth in his brown face. 'Well, there's always salvage,' he said, cheerfully.

The engine throbbed and burst into action and the boat almost disappeared in the surf. Dawn watched the small boat plough through the waves and clenched her hands, giving up a silent prayer for their safety. The waiting was terrible. There was no point in sending for an ambulance until it was certain that there was someone who needed it. Mike had taken a flare with him and promised to send it up when they reached the boat. He would send another if they found an injured person and she would then go to the nearest telephone to summon an ambulance and to tell the coastguard.

The wind moaned softly through the scrubby gorse on the cliff and in the distance, Dawn saw a flare from a boat far out to sea. No wonder the coastguard wanted to reserve their facilities for the worst accidents. There was nothing that anyone could do for the boat out there from a shore position, but here, they could cope, and God willing, be of some lasting use.

It seemed an age before the first flare lit the sky. In the smoky light, she saw the boat lying almost on its side, lifting and falling less now that the hungry waves were cheated by the tide. The pathetic sail still hung over the side and now she could see that the sailing boat had been dismasted. It was a cabin cruiser to take perhaps six or seven passengers and crew . . . a family boat. The possibilities were horrendous and she tried to take an objective view, keeping her mind on what she could do and not on the ifs and buts that might never happen.

'You might have waited for me.' Miles Stratton emerged from the darkness.

'Oh!' she said. 'You again.' She stared, but could see little of his features, having given her torch to Bruce to take with him on the boat. The moon made one of her rare and reluctant appearances. 'Shouldn't you be in bed?' she said.

'Not when there is work to do,' he said, in a voice as cool as her own. 'Believe me, I have no wish to be here, but I saw the flare and hurried down. Does it mean they've found someone?'

'No, I'm waiting for the next flare. If they want an ambulance, I have to telephone.'

'At least I can do that,' he said. 'This is a part of our equipment, supplied by the local police.' He pulled out a small radio and tugged at the aerial. 'Dolphin to base,' he called, and relayed the latest news. A flare went high above the rocks and they could see two men bending over a heap of clothes . . . or a body. The white paint of the boat was now plainly visible and the cut of the hull. 'Christ!' said Miles Stratton. 'That boat belongs to Stephanie's brother.'

'How many on it?' Dawn asked.

He came out of shock and radioed for an ambulance. 'No,' he said, 'we've no idea how many, but we know there's at least one.'

'Can we manage?' said Dawn. 'Shall I go up to the inn to fetch more muscle?'

'I doubt if you'll find any. Dave Attril will be out in the lifeboat investigating that flare and most of the other men will either be with him, manning the emergency radio, or just hanging about the coastguard waiting for news. There have been three boats sunk and two more on the rocks, tonight. It's usually bad in spring and autumn when the tides are high, but this was a freak even for spring. It's dying down now, but I doubt if the ferries will run tomorrow.'

'And if he needs to go across to the mainland?'

'We'll have to call on the services unless our plane can make it. They're working on it now.'

'Who is?'

'Stephanie for one.' He laughed. 'Don't tell me that you think she's a dizzy blonde, too?'

'I don't know her,' said Dawn. He couldn't have sounded more proud of her if he was married to her, she thought.

'She's an engineer with a flair for design, but she came up the hard way and isn't afraid of getting her hands dirty or losing a night's sleep in a good cause.'

'That's not unusual,' she said, sharply. 'Doctors and nurses do it all the time.'

'True . . . feeling tired?' he mocked.

'I've felt warmer and more rested,' she said. 'And if there is a casualty, I shall feel even worse by morning, I've no doubt.'

The tension between them was like thin glass stretched over a bowl. One tiny pressure out of place might send it shattering, releasing what kind of emotions?

A cry from the wreck came clearly through the spray and Mike staggered along the ridge, dragging a life raft on which was bound a figure.

Bruce followed, guiding the sled-like con-
veyance, so that it suffered as few knocks as
possible. Miles Stratton waded out, disregarding
the fact that the water came up to his thighs, to
help them over the last twenty yards, and within
minutes, Dawn was gazing down into the ashen
face of a young man with thick blond hair who
bore a decided resemblance to Stephanie. She
wrapped him in the insulating blanket that she
had begged from the hospital and went to put on
the car lights to guide the ambulance to the
scene. Miles Stratton was shivering as the cold
air cut through his soaking trousers and she
brusquely told him to get in the back seat of the
car and take off his wet clothes.

'Now you know why I brought some of Bruce's
things,' she said, with a certain amount of grim
satisfaction. 'Get changed at once unless you
want to be warded, too.'

'Best do as you're told, Doctor.' Mike
laughed. 'She'll have you stripped off if you
don't watch it. Put you in the shower she will.'

Miles Stratton opened his mouth to say something, but thought better of it. He meekly
vanished into the car while Dawn and Bruce
Tyley went with the ambulance men to see the
patient settled in the back. 'Drive the car, will
you, Dawn?' said Bruce. 'I'll go with them and
see him into bed. We can't make an examination
here.' He looked very anxious. 'It's Stephanie's

brother,' he said. 'God knows what she'll say when she hears.'

'Was he alone?'

'No sign of another passenger,' he said.

Dawn Campion had a sudden deep awareness that Bruce dreaded knowing who was on the boat with Jeff. His agonised expression told her all she wanted to know. 'It's all right, Bruce.' She laid a gentle hand on his arm as he waited his turn to get into the back with the ambulance man and the patient. 'She wasn't there.'

'How do you know?' He stared at her, his eyes suddenly in deep hollows of pain.

'She's working on the emergency plane. They had trouble with it today and she's been with Miles Stratton all afternoon.'

He tried to smile, but was nearer to tears. 'Bless you,' he murmured and took her into a bear-like hug that was gratitude, affection and sheer relief . . . but not love, and Dawn kissed his cheek before he went into the ambulance and away to the hospital.

She turned back to the car and saw Miles Stratton viewing her balefully. 'Have you changed?' she asked.

'I've borrowed his jeans and his sweater, and that smelly duffle coat,' he said, resentfully, 'but I refuse to wear another man's shoes.'

'His wouldn't fit you,' she said, and started up the engine. She adjusted the rear-view mirror and saw that Miles Stratton was staring at the back of her head. She ripped off the sailing cap and tossed it back to him. 'You're right . . . clothes are very personal . . . it's best to keep to one's own or to those worn by people one knows well.' She drove carefully and there was silence between them as they reached Casualty. 'I must see if I can help,' she said. 'The evening has gone and I shan't sleep now for hours.'

'You're not the only one,' he said. 'And I must find out how he is . . . and what his prognosis will be before I tell Stephanie that he is hurt.'

'Why you?' she said.

'I'm the obvious person to tell her,' he said. She recalled Bruce saying that Miles Stratton had pipped him in the competition for one lovely blonde, and her heart was heavy. Why couldn't Bruce tell her . . . why not Bruce, who loved her, too?

Poor Bruce . . . poor me, she thought, and wondered if life would ever be the same again for either of them. Perhaps they should team up and go back to Australia, to work and forget the two people who had such a hold over their hearts and destinies if they stayed within sight or sound of them in England.

The ambulance man folded his wet blankets, ready to take them and the oxygen back to the depot for replacements. He refused a cup of coffee, saying that they had another call to make, and warned them that they might expect two other bad casualties. 'A man and his wife were sitting in their car when a tree fell on it,' he said. 'Might go to Newport, but they'll be pretty full, I reckon.'

Miles Stratton went into the cubicle where Jeff Lawson lay, and looked down at the grey face and slack skin. He put a hand on the flaccid wrist and tried to find a pulse. Oxygen was already flowing in an attempt to oxygenate his blood. 'Is he alive?' whispered Dawn.

Dr Stratton left the bedside. 'Only just,' he whispered. 'Tyley is going to test his reflexes.'

For the next fifteen minutes, Sister Dawn Campion felt like an unwanted visitor. Both men and the night sister hovered round the casualty couch, and every neurological test within the scope of their facilities, was made to assess and diagnose the condition of the desperately ill man. At last, Bruce put down his stethoscope and faced Miles Stratton. 'What do you think, Miles? He should be in an intensive-care unit. I think he needs a decompression urgently.'

'Fractured base and fragments of the right temporal with possible involvement of the parietal.'

Bruce nodded.

'I know a bloke at East Grinstead who is the best,' said Miles Stratton. 'The sea is high with a rolling swell. Out of the question, and Air Sea

Rescue have their hands full.' He looked grimly at the chart. 'I'll have to tell Stephanie that the first patient using the plane is her brother.'

'I'll go with him,' said Bruce. He looked at Dawn. 'Will you come with me?'

'Yes,' she said. 'I'll get my pack and some things. Where do we pick up transport?' She felt icy calm now that she knew what to do and the sight of Bruce's tortured face filled her with compassion.

'Yes . . . you go, Sister. You should go together,' said Miles Stratton. His expression was unfathomable, but Dawn knew that he believed that she loved Bruce and this made it easier. He would never know that she wanted him to go with her and the patient . . . wanted him to be near her when she was sent on any anxious or dangerous mission she might be called on to do . . . wanted him . . . just wanted him as she had wanted no other person in her life.

'The hospital ambulance will take him to the plane on the old landing strip which they've cleared for our use. The transfer should take less than half an hour . . . a good flight with the wind behind you and no gusting now . . . I'll alert the theatre there so that he can go straight in.' Miles Stratton grinned. 'You'll have to come back by ferry. Take your sea-sick pills with you . . . it might be rough.'

'Don't worry, we'll stay the night, or what's

left of it. We can't catch a ferry until about eight, I believe,' said Bruce. He smiled with a little more conviction. 'Should be fun. Do you mind having breakfast with me, Dawn?'

The smile faded from Dr Stratton's face. 'Take care,' he said.

'Don't worry. Now that I know we can get him to the experts, everything will be fine,' said Bruce, but Dawn wondered if Miles was talking about the patient. What if she had breakfast with Bruce Tyley? What if she slept with him in a hotel in East Grinstead? It was no business of anyone but the two people concerned. Was Miles Stratton the type of man who couldn't bear to see other people pairing off, but was sure that he could do it? He would condemn anyone for falling in love . . . if they weren't fawning at his elegant feet.

'In that case, I'd better bring a toothbrush,' she said, demurely.

The telephone rang and Miles Stratton answered it. 'The pilot is ready, the plane is Okay and the ambulance is waiting. You've tested the oxygen cylinder?'

Dawn nodded. 'I've fetched my bag and the first-aid kit, the oxygen is full and we have spare blankets and hot-water bottles in case it's very cold, but I believe you would rather keep his temperature low at this time.'

'Fine.' He smiled and it was a ray of sunlight in

her cold heart. He bent to pick up her case and carried it to the ambulance, putting it with the other equipment. 'Take care,' he said, again. He looked deep into her eyes. 'Remember that this kind of work adds an unreal dimension to life . . . a heady sensation that can be misleading . . . and people have been known to do things out of character because they are elated.'

She could only gaze up at him, hypnotised by his eyes, his words and his nearness. He bent to kiss her lips, and she trembled. He almost pushed her into the vehicle.

'You see . . . it can happen to anyone . . . take care.'

CHAPTER SEVEN

'WHAT are you doing here Sister? Matron sent a message to say that you would be off until mid-afternoon.'

'She might have told you that, but she couldn't give me any messages where I was,' said Sister Dawn Campion, with a tired smile.

'You look terrible,' said Nurse Brody with a hint of malicious enjoyment. 'Were you air sick?'

'Nothing like that. In fact it was a much smoother flight than I thought possible after the storm we had here. By the time we were air-borne, the gusting had eased and we could manage quite well, without either the patient or Dr Tyley falling out!'

'How did you get on with Bruce Tyley?' Nurse Brody gave Dawn a sideways glance that told her just how much the breakfast table company had gossiped and speculated about the possible re-percussions of being in such close contact with the attractive and dangerous doctor.

'He was great,' said Dawn, warmly. 'I didn't know what a good doctor he is until last night. He didn't leave the patient for one moment and by the time we had charted every breath he took, or so it seemed, we were flying over the hospital at East Grinstead and the pilot was asking for permission to land. It was very strange,' said Dawn, 'almost unreal.' She sighed. 'It worked like a dream. We got on the plane and flew straight there, the ambulance was waiting and a police escort took us to the hospital at speed . . . quite like American TV extravaganzas, a stretcher trolley was waiting and he disappeared into the anaesthetic room while Bruce told the surgeon all the details and showed the wet-plates of the X-rays. It was almost as quick as taking a patient from one end of a huge hospital to the other, stopping only to change staff half way.'

'Did you see him after the operation?'

'No. He was still in intensive care this morning when we left to catch the first ferry.' She yawned. 'I think the most tedious part was the taxi ride from the ferry at Ryde across the Island. Not the nicest of weather and some of the smaller roads were flooded.'

'Are you going to bed?'

'I thought I'd come here first, in uniform, in case I was needed.' She smiled. 'I'm sorry if I did you out of the first trip, Nurse Brody. I know you were keen to take part, but I happened to be on the spot . . . only minutes after signing that I'd be on call.'

'I was disappointed when I heard that you had

gone, but when I came back here to find what was happening after we saw the flares go up when we were eating in the Smugglers, we had our share, too.'

'They said there might be some more casualties.'

'A couple crushed in their car under a fallen tree.'

'How are they? Did they stay here?'

'It was all go for a couple of hours. We had trouble with cross-matching blood for the man, who was a rare blood group, and the woman was hysterical.'

'Who took the cases?'

'Dr Hobart came in to help Dr Stratton. They stitched up a few gashes, set the woman's broken arm and sedated her and put the husband under observation, with query internal injuries.'

'That doesn't sound too good,' said Dawn. 'Has he gone to theatre yet?'

'No. He's been X-rayed and palpated and his pulse was down to normal the last time I heard from the ward. I think he was severely shocked and has a history of mild heart disease which might account for his thready pulse. His wife didn't help, screaming blue murder, when she was injured less than he was.'

'What is there to do here? Let's both get it clear and then we can rest in the office in case we are needed. You need a break as much as I do.'

'What happened? You were too late for the last ferry, I know. Did they give you a bed . . . or two, at the hospital?' the implied question was unmistakable.

'They offered me a bed and Bruce went with one of the doctors to his quarters,' Dawn said, sweetly. Now spread that around, she thought.

They worked quickly and quietly until all traces of the night's work had been washed away, the drums used were stacked for sterilising and fresh drums lay on the rack. Nurse Brody put on the kettle and brought a second comfortable chair from the corridor that also acted as a waiting area for relatives if a child or invalid was having treatment in outpatients. 'I don't know if this is a good idea,' said Nurse Brody.

'I agree. I feel as if my eyes are propped open with very sharp toothpicks. Perhaps some really strong coffee will help. Have you had breakfast?' Nurse Brody nodded. 'I had a sandwich with Bruce on the ferry, but that was years ago. I'm starving. If you make the coffee, I'll pop over to the cottage and get some food. I bought a whole veal pie, thinking I could use it for picnics when I walk on the Down. I can get half an hour's exercise like that every day if I don't go in to lunch, but this is an emergency!' Dawn picked up her cloak. 'Ketchup or pickle for you?' she called as she left the department.

'Pickle,' said Miles Stratton, lounging in the

doorway. 'No, don't let me detain you. I can see that you are engaged on yet another life-saving mission.' His face was drawn but his eyes sparkled. 'Mind if I bring in another chair . . . and beg a cup of coffee?'

Dawn hurried to her room and packed a picnic bag with the pie, some biscuits and relishes. A can of mushrooms and some fresh celery were added and she rushed back to find Dr Stratton stretched out in the low easy chair, his eyes half closed. Nurse Brody brought in the coffee and Dawn sliced up the pie.

'Wonderful,' murmured Miles Stratton. 'Last night I dreamed of veal pie when I was stitching up that scalp.' He put out a hand for his share.

'You're as bad as Dr Tyley. We say he can smell coffee and food from two hundred paces,' said Nurse Brody.

Dr Stratton grinned. 'He can't smell this. He's snoring away in his room. What did you do to him, Sister?'

'Me? I was too busy with my patient to do anything,' she said.

'And after?' The hand holding the piece of pie paused between plate and mouth.

'The kind people at the hospital gave us shelter for the rest of the night until we could catch the morning ferry back to the Island,' she said. 'Have you heard any news from East Grinstead?'

'Yes. I rang them just now and thought you might like to know. Jeff Lawson had surgery last night, as you possibly know.'

'Yes, we went with him to the theatre . . . to tell you the truth, I wanted to be sure his pulse was still beating when we handed him over.' The memory of his still greyness saddened her.

'They did a decompression and removed slivers of bone from the parietal bone, sucked out a large blood clot that was doing more damage than the fracture, and he began to respond almost immediately. As we got him there so soon, he stands a good chance of a full recovery with no lasting brain damage through cerebral starvation.'

'That's wonderful,' said Dawn, her eyes shining. 'I must confess that there were a couple of times on the flight when I thought he was dead.'

'It shows what we can do in a small way to help the existing services. It isn't perfect by any means. I want to be able to keep the plane ready to return staff to base. It must have taken hours to get back by public transport.' He smiled.

'Have you been to bed at all, Dr Stratton?' asked Nurse Brody.

'It wasn't worth it. After the two here last night, I kept in touch with East Grinstead so that I could pass on any messages,' he said.

'You rang his sister?' said Dawn. Of course. That was the reason for his shining eyes and his elation on hearing the news of the success of the operation. It must be wonderful, she thought, to be the first to tell the woman you love something that she needs to hear, something to make her weep tears of joy and relief . . . almost as satisfying as taking her in his arms to comfort her . . . to reassure her and to tell her he loved her.

'She was over the moon,' he said. 'It also made her even more keen to get on with this service. She's a wonderful person . . . practical and imaginative,' he said, then filled his mouth with some of his second slice of pie.

Beautiful, too, and very sophisticated, thought Dawn, unhappily. It isn't fair. Bruce loves her and so does Miles Stratton. Why can't she love Bruce instead of taking the one man who could make me a happy woman?

'That saved my life,' he said. 'I'm going to do a round and then go to bed for a couple of hours. I advise you two to do the same if you can. I know that Matron will agree to anything that doesn't upset the smooth working of the hospital.' He looked out at the lazily drifting clouds. 'There's a swell on the water, but the storm has gone, so we can be fairly sure that the hospital is quiet. I don't think there is a single bed left, which cuts out emergencies for a start.'

'It's an idea. We can still be on call if Nurse Brody sleeps in my cottage,' said Dawn.

'And when Stephanie Lawson comes back this

evening from East Grïnstead, I suggest that we all meet in the Smugglers Rest to toast the new service which got off to a good start even without all the refinements we thought might be needed.'

'She's going over today? It's a long journey and she must be tired. How can she do both journeys and be fresh enough to meet you tonight?' said Nurse Brody.

'She's flying. Did you know she has a pilot's licence? She's taking Francis Meadows' plane and coming back the same way.'

'Aren't you going with her?' asked Dawn.

'No. Bruce Tyley wanted to see Jeff and take notes for our records and, of course, he has a personal interest in seeing his patient.' He looked at her with dark-shadowed eyes and said, 'I expect you'd like to go too, but I suggest you postpone the trip until you are rested. Tyley is sleeping now, so he'll be bright and bushy tailed.' His smile was half-hearted, as if he still disapproved of his colleague.

'More coffee?' said Dawn, and her eyelashes lay like dark moths on her pale cheeks. 'You'll let us know any further news, please?'

'Of course, and when he's fit, I know that Jeff will want to meet you. We must arrange something.'

The perfect, polite but non-committal phrase, thought Dawn, but would they bother with her once he was well and strong and Miles Stratton was married to Stephanie? The circle would be small and warm and totally exclusive.

'I'd like that,' she said, softly.

'I'll see you both tonight at nine in the bar. I expect there will be a few tales being told of the storm. One faction will be telling of storms in the past and the other about how this was the worst in living memory!'

'And will Miss Lawson be there?' asked Nurse Brody. 'She will be able to give us the latest news.'

'I don't know. She'll ring me later.' He stood tall as if to unkink his joints, then walked slowly away, his well-set shoulders proud even through his weariness.

'Clear away and I'll ring matron's office to tell her that we're all ready here for anything that comes in, but we'll be in my cottage if she needs us.'

Over the telephone, Sister Dawn Campion had to give every detail of her adventure during the night and an account of how she returned in the morning. Matron was delighted and very co-operative and gave her a free hand to plan her work to fit in with the new arrangements. 'Just keep me informed, Sister, so that I can contact you. Sleep well, you've earned a rest.'

The two weary girls dragged their tired feet across to the cottage and pulled the curtains across the windows to shut out the brittle glare of

the sun. 'It's a lovely day,' said Dawn, sleepily.
'It's such a waste to sleep it away,' but the next
thing she heard was her alarm shrilling beside
her head, bringing her back from a deep pit of
sleep.

She yawned and glanced at her watch, unable
to believe that she had been to sleep for more
than a few minutes. 'Brody!' she called. 'It's six
o'clock.'

She ran across to her kitchen and put water on
to boil, then hurried into the bathroom to take a
refreshing shower, telling Brody that she would
be only five minutes and that she could follow her
while she dressed and made tea.

'Just as well we ate something earlier. We
missed lunch and there are only a few biscuits left
after last night,' Brody said, as they sat sipping
tea and eating hot toast and honey. 'I feel a
hundred per cent better, and I'm looking forward to seeing them all at the Smugglers this
evening.'

'I don't think I'll go,' said Dawn. 'I'll check up
and make up my day book in my office, have
supper in the dining room and have an early
night.'

'But Dr Stratton asked us to go.' It was clear
that Brody was appalled at anyone refusing an
invitation from the wonderful Dr Stratton, and
had possibly not received one from him before
today.

'There will be plenty of people there. They won't notice if I'm not there.' She laughed. 'I shall have to listen to it all many times when people like Mike Carter come in here. By the way, has he been up for a dressing?'

'He came before the night staff left, saying he wanted to do some beach-combing today and would be fishing later. He treats this place as his private clinic, but he makes me laugh and I can never tell him off.'

'I think he earns a little spoiling. Last night he was marvellous. To see him climb over those awful rocks you'd never think he weighed as much as he does or drinks as much as he seems to do in the Smugglers. He was as confident as a cat and as fast. Dr Tyley was almost as good, but he took his pace from Mike.'

'You aren't completely blinded by his charm, Sister?'

'I don't accuse Mike of charm!'

'Not Mike . . . Dr Tyley. He rates next to Dr Stratton in my book. We're lucky to have two dishy men round the place and not a collection of spotty, humourless medics who think that women are merely nursing or physio staff or potential gynae cases.'

'They may look good, but is their attitude all that different?'

'You should know, Sister,' said Brody with a wicked wink.

'I think you're light headed . . . "elated and acting out of character" is what your esteemed Dr Stratton would say, Nurse.'

'Is that why he kissed you by the ambulance, Sister?' she asked, sweetly. 'Was he acting out of character?'

'Completely. He was merely glad that I was helping the brother of a woman he holds in very high esteem,' she said. 'And if you have *quite* finished trying to add two and two together to make six, I'll get back to my office and do some work before reporting everything hopefully all clear for Night Sister. It's our evening for autoclave duty, so I'll bid you a hot and steamy evening, Nurse Brody!'

'Oh, help! I'd forgotten. I'll get one lot in before supper and do two batches of gloves for the theatre in case they need them,' said Brody, hurrying off to the rack to collect the first of the packed drums awaiting steam sterilising.

Dawn wandered back to her office. She was rested but still felt a little weak from the excitement of the previous night. The weather had changed, mocking her with its light breeze, and gentle warmth, and making the Island once more a place of beauty and gentleness. A line of gulls on a roof told a tale of further storms at sea as they faced the breeze and ruffled feathers that still gleamed wet from the spray. It would be Easter in a few days' time and she realised that she had not given a thought to the fact that she had the whole of Easter Sunday off, Sunday, and Easter Monday morning, quite by accident and only because the off-duty rota worked that way.

She wondered if Isobel Horner would visit her, and found it difficult to tie up the two separate parts of her life. Most of her friends lived and worked in London, and yet, this small hospital held more for her at the moment than any other place on earth. It would be good to see Isobel and to show her some of the Island. I'll telephone her tonight, she thought, and ask her to come early to avoid the rush on the ferry when hordes of weekenders crowd them to get to holiday chalets, hotels or relatives living on the Island.

The evening passed without incident and birds sang by the open window of the office as if spring was well advanced and summer just round the corner. If Easter was fine, it would be fun to show Isobel all the tiny bays that were quiet and free from strangers even during school holidays, and it was with a sensation of pleasant antici-pation that she dialled the number that might find her friend off duty at Beatties.

'Sister Horner? Just a minute and I'll see if she's in her room,' said a voice, not quite manag-ing to hide her disappointment. Dawn smiled. How many times had nurses hovered near the telephone in the nurses' hostel in the hope of receiving a call from the latest heart throb, only to find the message was for someone living two floors up and at the other end of a corridor?

'Sister Horner here,' said a breathless voice.

'It's Dawn. I thought I'd check with you in case you can manage a visit this Easter.'

'I hoped you'd ring. I have the weekend off and I want to see my cousin who lives in the New Forest, so I can easily combine the two visits while I'm in the South of England.'

'I can give you a bed,' said Dawn.

'I'll come on Friday and stay over-night and get across on the last ferry on Saturday so that I'll miss the Easter Sunday and Monday rush. I'd better stay with the family for the real Easter holiday as they like to go to church and want me to join them.'

'That's wonderful, I shall look forward to it.'

'Don't tell me you have to rely on old friends to fill your time?' Isobel laughed. 'Have you met my friend . . . the one I was forbidden to mention in case you disliked him? I hope he's included in your plans. I'm dying to meet him again and to hear about this flying scheme.'

'You mean Dr Stratton?'

'Of course I do.' Isobel was annoyed. 'You know very well I mean Miles. What have you done? You didn't greet him with that "I've gone off men" look, did you?'

'No, the first snub came from him and proved

that it isn't safe to expect to make friends with people whose praise has been sung too loudly.'

'Oh, well, I expect you'll tell me all about it when we meet.'

'There's nothing to tell. I have met him, he is a good doctor and you will probably meet him, but he's far too busy professionally and emotionally to bother with me. He thinks I'm quite efficient . . . and that's a revised opinion, but he also finds me rather comic, with is *not* good for my ego. So when you come, don't expect me to be arm-in-arm, with ecstatic expressions. Didn't you know he has a lady love?' She laughed shortly. 'You should do your homework, Bella. I'll meet the Lymington ferry about noon . . . is that the one?'

'Fine. I'll drive down and leave my car in the car park. How do we get to your place? Is it far?'

'No, not far. We can bus most of the way or I might be able to lay on transport. I know someone with a car who might help out.'

'Ah . . . so there *is* a man?'

'Isobel! I wonder I bother with you! I have got to know a lot of people, most of them very pleasant, but there is no one man. Please believe that and don't come here pairing me off with everyone I speak to.'

'I might have known you'd gather some talent round you, Dawn. I'm glad to know you haven't lost your touch.'

"See you on Friday,' said Dawn. She sat for a

minute in silence. How can I convince Bella that neither of the good-looking men here have any lasting interest in me? Even Bruce, who thought he was falling in love with me, isn't really serious. He just needed someone to bolster his morale after Dr Miles Stratton took Stephanie from under his nose. She smiled, wryly. Poor Bruce. It must have been difficult to travel with the woman he really loves, in a tiny plane, knowing her to be in love with another man. 'We have a lot in common,' she murmured.

'Finished with the telephone?' said Irene Meadows. 'I want to ring Francis. He should be back by now and he can meet us all this evening. I hear that Miles is planning quite a get-together.'

'Is he? I wasn't sure that I would be rested enough to go, but Nurse Brody seems to think I will be committing a sin if I stay away.'

'And so you would. You are a part of the team and you've shown that you can help. Believe me, Dawn, I think we're very lucky to have you on our staff. Bruce was singing your praises.'

'He's awake at last?' Dawn laughed. 'He went straight to bed for a while, then had to get up to fly to the mainland with Miss Lawson. He must feel half dead.'

'When I saw him just now, he looked very bright and relaxed.'

'It's a wonder he hasn't come round, scrounging coffee and food.' Dawn smiled. 'I think we cleaned out his store of cake and biscuits.'

'He's had a snack with Stephanie in the other cottage and he's doing a ward round now to make sure he can go to the local without worrying about patients. I think this scheme has done him good. He is much more interested in the hospital as a whole.'

'Amazing what a beautiful blonde can do,' said Dawn.

'I rather thought that you might have had something to do with the change in his attitude.'

'I doubt it,' said Dawn. 'You over-estimate my influence, Irene.'

'I thought you made a very deep impression on one or two people here.' Irene smiled and picked up the telephone receiver. 'I'll call in for you later,' she said. 'Put on your best bib and tucker and we should have a very good evening.'

Dawn heard her talking rapidly and laughing as soon as her husband answered the telephone. It must be wonderful to have such sympathy and rapport with another human being . . . to love someone wholeheartedly and to be loved in return. She went to her room and opened her wardrobe. What's the use? she thought. It doesn't matter what I wear. It might give the locals a bit of a thrill to see their casualty sister dressed up and looking pretty, but was it worth the effort to impress Mike and Dave and that crowd?

She put the skirt back in her wardrobe and then took it out again, suddenly ashamed. Surely it was worth dressing up a little if it gave pleasure to the men who had worked so hard all night for others? She recalled the scene on the rocks when Mike Carter ran cat-like across the weed-covered ridge to help the man lying unconscious on the stricken boat, and knew that Dave and his life-boat crew had saved the men on the trawler that had foundered by the undercliff. These were the men who mattered, not the men she might find more attractive but unattainable. The local people were her friends now and she owed them anything she might have to give . . . efficient hospital treatment, comfort, and if it did Mike good to eye her legs . . . what did it matter? She chuckled, remembering that Nurse Peebles had viewed Mike with a great deal of favour when he came to Casualty. I ought to ask her to come tonight, she thought.

But it wasn't her party. She had been invited because she was one of the team who had helped Jeff Lawson, not for any other reason, and it was none of her business who was invited. She showered and dressed in the full skirt of ethnic tweed, glowingly coloured and softly draped. She teamed it with a pure silk shirt that followed the lines of her body and tucked into the slim waist-band, picking out the subtle shade of grey that was in the tweed with the soft gold and cinnamon. Bronze shoes that had lain unworn since before her car accident added to the effect and she brushed her hair until it shone like ripe chestnuts and amber. A Victorian locket left to her by her grandmother sat sweetly in her cleavage, the heavily embossed gold heavy against her creamy skin. Inside, there was a lock of hair from a lover . . . friend or relative, now long dead, and in the other tiny frame was a blank space, waiting for her own memory . . .

Irene knocked on the door. 'Don't worry about walking. We have a lift.' Dawn picked up her small handbag and keys and went out to join her. She slung a thick woollen coat over her shoulders, but the air was warm and she hoped that in the Smugglers Rest it would be hot enough to sit in the thin silk shirt.

'Good girl!' said Irene with approval. 'Come on, the car's waiting. Nurse Brody is already hogging the front seat and looking like the cat with the cream.'

'I know she was looking forward to this. She doesn't have much social life,' said Dawn.

The bar was packed with fishermen all talking at once and comparing stories that would, as the evening progressed, become taller and saltier and slide into the folk history of the region.

'There's Sister . . . come on and sit by me,' said Dave Attril.

'Sorry, Dave . . . we'll see you later. We have

a party in the other room, but I want to hear you play if you can manage it.' He grinned and she was glad that she had made an effort to be sociable and to dress up for the evening. Dawn sat by Francis Meadows and liked him at once. Bruce had arrived and was sitting with Stephanie, the two fair heads close together and she was laughing. Dawn smiled but her lips were stiff. Stephanie was looking softly at Bruce as if she was attracted to him. Wasn't it enough that she had ensnared Miles Stratton? She didn't look as if she was the kind of woman to play one man against another, but now she was smiling and showing Bruce a soft side to her nature that should by right be shared with the man she really loved and not with the man who had happened to spend a few hours with her while she visited her brother in hospital.

Dawn was greeted with enthusiasm by Bruce who crossed the room and kissed her cheeks.

'Have a good trip?' she asked.

'Great! Jeff's fine . . . hardly recognise him as the same guy. You must meet him some time. Stephanie heard all about you and she wants to arrange something, soon.'

There it was again . . . the casual invitation that meant nothing and needn't be followed up. 'Like surfing in Australia?' she said, softly. He blushed. 'I'm glad he's all right,' she said, and laughed. What did it matter that Bruce loved

Stephanie? This was no time to play dog-in-a-manger when Bruce was so obviously in love with Stephanie, and if she was honest, Dawn had no claim on him nor did she want one. 'Stephanie looks very happy,' she said. 'You look good together, Bruce.'

His eyes searched hers for laughter and found none. 'Bless you,' he said . . . 'But you must still come surfing.'

'If I'm passing,' she said. He bent to kiss her lips, briefly, in gratitude for her understanding and everyone was too occupied with their neighbours to notice. Even Stephanie had turned away to greet the man who had thought up the idea of the ambulance service. She was calling to Miles who stood at the door, watching the people in the room, missing nothing.

'Bruce,' Stephanie turned as he began to make his way back to his seat by her side. 'Miles has arrived.' She looked over the heads of the people seated at the small tables. 'Over there,' she said. 'They've put a microphone there by that table in case you want to say a few words.' He nodded and pushed between the tables to the seat next to Dawn Campion.

'May I?' he said, and the jasper-dark eyes were sad.

'Of course.' Dawn gave him a brilliant smile and moved a little so that he could squeeze by into his chair. Her heart was filled with turmoil.

To have him near her, so that his hand brushed against her silken shoulder, was breathless enough, but to feel the tautness of his thigh against her leg in the restricted space of the crowded room made her dizzy with emotion.

'Are you all right?' he said. 'You look a little flustered.' He glanced across the room. 'I'll change places with Bruce if you like . . . that is, if Stephanie doesn't mind.'

'No,' she said. 'This is fine.' She made an effort to appear normal. 'You haven't told me about Jeff Lawson yet . . . Bruce only said he was all right.' Talk . . . laugh and make it seem as if she enjoyed his company in a casual way so that he would never suspect how she loved him . . . talk and joke and try to take the hurt from his eyes made by the beautiful blonde who now ignored him and laughed with his rival, Bruce Tyley.

'I hear you did very well,' he said, and smiled. She leaned forward and the heavy locket slid from its hiding place between her breasts. Her fingers toyed with it and she bit the chain, repeating the habit she had acquired as a child. He put out a hand and took the locket on to the palm of his hand. 'You'll ruin those pretty teeth if you do that,' he said. 'What is it? It's heavier than it looks.'

She leaned back, taking the trinket from him, unable to bear the touch of his hand on her throat. 'It's been in the family for ages.'

'Has it anything inside. What secrets have you hidden there?'

'None of my own,' she said, sadly. 'I have no keepsakes.' She opened the front and showed him the lock of dark hair, still shining after the generations who had examined it and wondered. 'I don't know who gave this to the woman who owned it, originally.'

'No lock of fair hair?' he said, lightly, but his mouth had an edge of bitterness.

'I think fair hair would look odd,' she said. 'I shall pass it on to my niece when I'm very old . . . and she can fill it with a lock of hair from the man she marries.'

'I'm glad it won't be fair,' he said.

She looked down, unable to meet the pain that she knew he hid behind the sombre gaze. She took a deep breath. 'I believe we have a mutual friend,' she said, determined to change the subject and to salvage something from the evening before they sank into complete misery. 'I was talking to Isobel Horner from Beatties this evening. She is coming to see me on Friday.'

'That's wonderful! I didn't realise that you knew each other.' He smiled. 'She's a wonderful person. Every student at Beatties has to thank her for some kindness. She shields all us poor men from the terrors of outpatients and the students from the wrath of consultants.'

'I'm meeting the noon ferry at Yarmouth,' she said.

'That's good. I can help you there. I have to collect some equipment from that ferry, so I can bring you both back here.'

'But . . . it will take up your time,' she said, weakly. 'I could borrow a car, I expect.'

'No need,' he said, crisply. 'Unless you can't tolerate my company for so long.' He shrugged. 'I know you resent me for some reason or other and draw away as if I am infectious, but I assure you that it will give me pleasure to be of use to . . . Bella.' He picked up his glass. 'It's time I proposed a toast to the new service and the people who work with it.'

CHAPTER EIGHT

Dawn shrugged off the light anorak she wore over her cream cord jeans and black lambswool sweater. 'It's very warm,' she said. 'You must have gone out early to sniff the air.' She gave an envious glance at the well-cut cotton jeans and red-checked brushed cotton shirt that Dr Miles Stratton wore with negligent elegance.

'I've a heavy jacket in the back,' he said. 'It doesn't do to trust the weather so early in the season. Just because the sea is dead calm and the sky is blue, it leads us to think it will be like it for ever, and we all know what happened that night of the storm.'

'Don't,' she said, and her face tightened. 'Thank goodness that Jeff Lawson is going to be all right.'

'Yes, Stephanie went over again yesterday with Tyley and they came back laughing.' He glanced at the sunlight dancing on the auburn hair at his side, but Dawn showed no sign of being upset at the fact that Bruce Tyley had deserted her in favour of the lovely Stephanie. 'Open the window if it's too warm in the car,' he said. He leaned over and touched the handle that

163

would raise or lower the window. 'That one . . . or you'll fall out,' he said, smiling.

'I'm not that daft,' she said with a hint of irritation. It was bad enough to sit with the man she loved and to know that it meant nothing to him, but need his hand fall warm on hers by accident? Need he be quite so devastatingly handsome in the rugged, casual clothes that would make lesser men look like peasants?

'It's very still,' she said. 'In fact, when I looked out this morning, the coast road was slightly misty.' She tried to concentrate on the day ahead. 'I hope that Bella caught the boat. She would have to get up early to drive down from London and if there is mist on the motorway, I know she will be very uneasy.'

'Once she's here, she needn't worry. There are plenty of people to give lifts, or you could take her by rail. It's amazing what can be seen of the Island in that way.'

The car slowed as they reached Yarmouth and it was difficult to find a parking space close to the harbour. 'Let's leave it here and walk. We've plenty of time and Irene would be pleased with me if I made you take exercise,' he said. They strolled along by the moored yachts and stopped to watch a party of six, dressed in crew-necked sweaters and grubby trousers, preparing to take out a cabin cruiser. 'Great fun,' said Miles Stratton.

'I did a bit of sailing when I was here a long time ago, but I haven't had the opportunity since,' Dawn said.

'We must do it this summer, before I go into the RAF.'

Her heart seemed to lurch. It was happening again. The casual half-invitation that would lead to nothing but made the perfect polite way out of any involvement.

'That would be fun,' she said, as if she believed him.

'You really would enjoy it?' His eyes held a warm pleasure in the jasper depths. 'Then we'll make up a party.'

The hooter on the ferry came over the water as the outward-bound boat left the harbour for the mainland. 'We should be there waiting, or she will wonder if she's being met and might take a taxi,' said Dawn. The incoming ferry came in through a veil of mist that swirled in eddying patches over the water. 'It's coming down a bit,' said Dawn. 'Bella will be biting her nails if it's been like that all the way.'

'Wait a minute.' Miles stopped at the booking office and looked down at a large blackboard outside the door. 'I think that's for you,' he said.

Dawn read a crudely scribbled message asking Miss Campion to enquire at the desk. She hurried inside, pushing past the people streaming off the ferry after the last of the cars. The man behind the desk handed her a message written on a brightly-coloured post-card view of Lymington which was all that Bella could find in a hurry. 'Please ring me at this number, Dawn, so that I know you received this message.' Dawn smiled. I couldn't very well acknowledge it if I *hadn't* received it, she thought. 'I came down through the most terrible mist,' the message went on, 'and I can't face crossing water in fog. I've decided to stay with my relatives in the New Forest for the whole of Easter, but if it clears, could you and Miles come over to see me?'

Dawn passed the card across without a word.

'Poor Bella,' he said and laughed. 'Quite the most efficient sister at Beatties, and yet she's scared of a little mist.' He grinned. 'I suppose we all have our weak spots. If we go sailing together, we shall find them.'

Not if I can help it, thought Dawn, fervently. Never, never must he know that he is my weak spot or I'd die of humiliation. 'Come on, we've time for coffee in the Bull before we go back, unless you have other plans?' she said, lightly.

'I've lots of other plans, but none I can put into action now, unfortunately,' he said and his eyes were once more serious.

And I know for a fact that Stephanie and Bruce have gone to Chale this morning, together, she thought. He knows it too, and can do nothing to prevent them being together.

The Bull was almost full of people, fresh from the ferry, anxious to sample the atmosphere of the ancient harbour and the fascinating little square full of provision shops, chandlers and other sailing needs. One woman was proudly showing her friend an old lamp she had bought, and of all things, six green glass floats. Dawn sat quietly, watching the odd collection of clothes that some people thought were suitable for a holiday by the sea in early spring, and Miles Stratton seemed content to sit beside her, occasionally making a remark, but for the most part following her gaze and smiling when she found something amusing. It was a good feeling and one that made her know how it could be with him if he loved her.

The window of the bar was almost opaque with mist and the passing crowds were shadows on the glass. 'Come on, let's get back and I'll take you for lunch to the Smugglers.' He waved aside her protests. 'You must feel an anti-climax after gearing your entire weekend round Bella. I was hoping to take you both to lunch, so I *do* have the time to spare.'

They walked back to the car and the boats in the harbour were fast becoming grey wraiths under a sun that battled to dispel the veil that was fast blotting out its light. 'Just as well Bella didn't come if it stays like this. With the suddenly warmer weather, this mist can stay for quite a

while,' said Miles Stratton. 'At least the risk of
people being caught on the cliffs and developing
hypothermia is less.' He frowned. 'But with all
these people who don't know the tides, the risk
of being cut off because they can't see the tide
race is greater.'

The mist swirled in fantastic spirals of witches'
cloaks and the sound of the sea as they came to
the Smugglers was eerie and almost impossible
to pinpoint, through the dull barrier fast forming
on the shore. Patches of light showed through
with bright sunlight, as if some of the cliff-top
hadn't heard that it must draw up its blankets.

'Let's walk to the end and see some real
waves,' said Dawn. 'Poor Bella was looking
forward to seeing some spray over the rocks and
this part of the Island is the only place where it is
always fairly rough.' She laughed. 'Bella is one
for quoting poetry at the strangest times. She
stood and quoted Tennyson, watching the boats
on the Serpentine one day! Of all things . . .
"Break, break, break, on thy cold grey stones,
oh sea!"'

He looked out at the mist on the water. '"And
I would that my tongue could utter The thoughts
that arise in me . . ."'

'Do you know much of his?' She was shaken
by the solemnity of his voice when he capped
her quotation. Did all things, even snippets of

poetry, make him think dark thoughts about the woman he loved?

He chuckled, breaking the tension. 'I know all the important bits like . . . "In the Spring a young man's fancy lightly turns to thoughts of love".'

'Did he write that?'

'Locksley Hall . . . and there are many beautiful lines in that long poem.' He was close to her, his dark eyes brooding with controlled passion. His hand brushed the dew of mist from her bright hair and found the gentle line of her cheek and his lips on hers were firm and warm and vaguely of the sea. A bird called, far out, as if lost for ever . . . was it an albatross with the spirit of a lost mariner crying for lost life . . . lost love? Tears streamed down her face as he kissed her again and gazed down into her troubled face. 'He lived here and knew it well. He wrote of love and suffering and sacrifice. Don't look back, Dawn . . . can't you forget the man who brought those tears to your eyes?'

He was being gentle, trying to make her forget Bruce's kiss, trying to boost her morale by showing that she was attractive to men.

'I always weep when people read beautiful lines,' she said, dashing away the tears.

He held her still, his shoulder strong as the rock beneath them and his heart pounding like a distant tide. 'Don't let the sands run out for you, Dawn. Look outward and believe in yourself.'

'I know what I want.' But she knew that she could never tell him. 'Aren't you the one who needs to look in other directions,' she said, boldly. 'I know that Stephanie is very beautiful, but there must have been other women in your life?'

His grip tightened, but he made no reply, and when she looked up she knew that he hadn't heard what she said. His dark eyes were strained to see through a thick bank of fog that hid the edge of the cliff. 'Did you hear it?'

'I heard a bird call,' she said, 'and, of course, the sea is louder here, now that the tide is coming in fast.'

'The tide! Listen!' He shook her gently, as if that would sharpen her hearing. 'Listen . . . there it is again.'

From the void came a thin cry that could be that of a gull, but it held a panic that no free-flying bird experienced. 'Where can it be?' Dawn broke free and took a step forward, but was seized and dragged back again.

'Don't be a fool. The edge is nearer than you think.' Once more she had the refuge of his arms and she sensed his breath close to her cheek, his lips on her hair. It would be so easy to turn and fling herself into his arms and to demand his love, to the exclusion of everything, the fog, the fact that he loved Stephanie . . . and the cry that brought her to sanity.

'Where's the path? I seem to remember a track along the edge that went down through some brambles. It's overgrown but possible if we go carefully.'

'I remember it too. They say it was once an old way down to the cove and the jetty. It lies in a direct line to the Smugglers' Rest and would have been useful for a mule track with contraband.' He held her hand tightly and went cautiously forward, staring out into the white blanket and trying to listen for further sounds. They came to a thick clump of gorse and bramble, prickly with young shoots and growing almost over the crumbling path. 'Wait,' he ordered and Dawn sat on the top and watched him try to push through the mass of prickles.

'Good thing you put that coat on,' she said. 'I think you should let me go. I'm smaller and can scramble through.'

'We don't know if the path is still there. Some of the cliffs round here have been eroded.' His confident voice faltered. 'Damn!' he said.

'What is it?' She bent forward anxiously and then bit her lip to stop the giggle that threatened to surface. 'My granny used to say I looked like an owl in an ivy bush when I was untidy . . . but this is ridiculous.' The elegant thick hair was caught on a clump of gorse and the more he pulled away the tighter it held.

'*Do* something . . . cut me free . . . but do something,' he said.

Dawn fumbled for her nail scissors and wriggled down to his level. Quietly, as if the person below was giving up hope, another cry came to them and Miles tried to tug free. 'Ouch!' he said. She carefully separated the shining dark strands and cut as little as possible close to the bush. He pulled free and rubbed his head. 'Good. You haven't done a complete Delilah hair-cut. Can you follow, carefully?'

Dawn tied up her head in the silk scarf she carried in the pocket of her jacket and bent to follow him. On the bush was a lock of hair and she paused long enough to prise it free, taking with it thorns and young leaves. Carefully, she put it all in her pocket and followed him down into the mist.

'Here,' he called. They looked down to a ledge just wide enough for the boy who lay on it. He was moving feebly and his hands fluttered as if trying to signal. Miles looked at the high-water marks on the rocks. 'He'll be covered if we leave him there. I'll stay with him while you get someone with a boat to go round and take him. He's hurt. Can you fetch my bag from the car and put it in the boat and send a blanket, too?'

She nodded and slid back swiftly, running to

the Smugglers Rest to alert the proprietor and to tell Mike Carter who was leaning on the bar talking, just what they had found.

'Durned overner, I reckon. They come here and never learn nothing.' He grinned. 'I'll get the boat. Doc's down there, is he?' She nodded and went to fetch the doctor's bag. Mike was starting the engine when she thrust bag and blankets into the boat. 'Best wait, Sister. Get the ambulance and tell them the old jetty. There isn't room for more than three of us.'

Once more she went back to the Smugglers and began to know how wives and sweethearts must feel while they waited for their men to return from the sea.

It seemed an age but couldn't have been more than half an hour before she heard the chugging of the outboard motor through the mist. Other men had gathered and the ambulance bell cut through the silence as the driver came carefully into sight, with all lights blazing. Dawn ran to the boat and watched the men transfer the injured youth to the ambulance. Blood dripped from a wound at the back of his head and when she felt his pulse it had the same lack of tension and slow beat that Jeff had when she watched over him on the journey to the hospital.

'I'm afraid so.' Miles looked down at her. 'He fell down the cliff when trying to reach a bird's nest. Silly young idiot.' His anger was real but

Dawn sensed that it was, like her own, directed against the stupidity of risking a life just to break the law and search for protected birds. For the patient in his present state there could be nothing but professional care and compassion. 'There may be a bed nearer than East Grinstead, but I do know the man there and we have an arrangement for these cases, as he lives near the hospital and doesn't have to be summoned from London or any of the other specialist centres. I'd like to get him there as quickly as possible.'

'But how?' A circle of anxious faces waited for his decision.

'We'll have to fly him out.' He turned to the ambulance driver. 'Would you get through to your base and ask them to alert the hospital? I'll fetch a few things and join you by the entrance to Casualty and we can all proceed to the plane from there.'

'But do you know if there's a pilot available?'

'Francis left the ambulance plane on the old runway so that we could measure up for lockers and make notes about equipment. It's tanked up and ready, but still a little basic in its finish.' He looked at Dawn's anxious face. 'I'm quite a good pilot, believe it or not.'

'But . . . you can't fly in this. The fog is getting thick and you'd never find your way.'

'Ever heard of radio?' The level brows lifted

and the slightly sardonic expression pulled her back from saying too much. 'I can do it if I am sure that the patient is being well cared for in the back. It will need all my concentration to fly and I have to be very sure of any help I have.'

She half turned away, sure that he wanted to make her understand that she would not be suitable to undertake the mission with him.

'Who have you in mind? Shall I ring the hospital or have you time to get a nurse from Newport?'

'There isn't time,' he said. 'He's still bleeding and we can't do much more than mop up and keep him quiet and see that his lungs have enough oxygen. Run and get your emergency pack and some extra clothes. I'll pick you up in five minutes and we can follow the ambulance to the plane in my car.' He smiled. 'Cheer up,' he said. 'I promise not to do a victory roll or anything exciting.'

'You really want me to come?'

'You'll do,' he said. 'Bring a toothbrush.'

Dawn picked her way through the mist patches and was glad that she had the emergency pack ready. She gathered up her toilet bag and stuffed a nightdress into her holdall with her make-up kit, paused to think if she'd forgotten anything and picked up the heavy gold locket that she had left lying on the dressing table. She slipped it on over her sweater and the weight was somehow comforting, a kind of good-luck token that would protect them.

He was waiting, the mist swirling about his dark head, and when they reached the plane and the patient was safely on the stretcher, she glanced down to watch him climb up to the pilot's seat, like a young and handsome pilot from World War II with a leather jacket over his thick sweater and a long scarf wound round his neck. 'Everything okay?' he called.

'Fine,' she said, firmly hiding the shake in her voice. 'I'm just renewing the bandage so that I can judge the blood loss and be able to see it stopping.'

'Good girl,' he said.

'Oxygen on and I'm keeping a ten-minute check on his pulse,' she said. 'Go ahead and I'll not bother you unless there's an emergency.' It was quiet and calm in the cabin and she felt confident that if anyone could get them safely to the mainland, it would be Miles Stratton.

The engine roared and the mist parted to let them lift into the air. Eddies of fog cut across by bars of sunlight were more confusing than a consistent mist, but the small plane pointed in a north-easterly direction with a bearing of 62 degrees towards Chichester, and kept doggedly on course under the firm hands of the pilot. From time to time, Dawn heard him communicating with Air Traffic Control who gave him clearance over the coast and immediate landing permission on the small runway nearest to the hospital. Already, Dawn knew that the staff would be waiting, ready to cope with whatever came to them, but until they were safely in hospital, the casualty was her responsibility.

'Stay quietly on the bed,' she said, clearly. The lad was muttering and trying to move his legs. He turned his head from side to side as if a stinging insect was buzzing round his ears. She put a soothing hand on his brow and found it cold and clammy. His pulse rate was going up and she knew that he was still losing blood through the scalp wound. It was impossible to put pressure on the wound in case there were fragments of bone that might become dislodged and imbedded in some vital centre of the brain. Urgent surgical treatment was needed and he was becoming more and more restless. The intravenous plasma that was running slowly into a vein in his arm was in danger of being dragged out, and she held his arm firmly and talked in a soft voice to calm him.

She glanced at the notes that had been hastily started in the ambulance and saw that he had already had a strong sedative to counteract his cerebral irritation. She held on, soothing and hoping that her calm words could get through to him while all the time she was conscious of the all-embracing fog and the difficulties of the pilot.

'Not long now,' she said, but whether it was to comfort the patient or to reassure herself, she couldn't tell. She blinked as she stared out at the fog. Was it her imagination or were there landing lights? She had no time to look further. The patient was threshing about again and she was hard pressed to keep him on the stretcher, even though he was strapped to it and the stretcher had cot-sides. Breathless, she hung on, talking and trying to hold his hand. He lurched over, trying to lie on the side where the intravenous was sited, and she tried to roll him back, gently. The chain of her locket caught in a strut and she felt it snap but could do nothing to retrieve it.

'All right?' The door opened and Dawn glanced back at the man who came into the cabin.

'Are we down?' she said, surprised to see Miles Stratton.

'Didn't you feel the bump?'

'Not a thing. I was too busy . . . oh, no you don't,' she said, making a grab at the patient. 'He's been a bit of a handful. Can we get him out of here?'

Willing hands lifted the stretcher on to the waiting ambulance and the police sirens filled the air, lights bounced off the fog and the ambulance drove swiftly and carefully under escort to the safety of the hospital.

Miles leaned against the wheel of the undercarriage. 'I'm not sorry to end up in one piece.' He looked at her, smiling, slowly. 'You do know you have blood on your hair and dirt round your eyes from the fog?'

'I know I must look a sight,' she said, suddenly tired.

'Quite a sight,' he said.

'What do we do now?' She peered through the fog. 'Do we just sit in the plane until the fog lifts? Have they abandoned us?' She tried to sound unconcerned, but a kind of delayed shock was making her legs weak.

'We can clear up in there and wait for a car I asked them to send for us.' He climbed up and put a hand down to help her. 'Come on. Let's get everything ready for the next one. Dirty dressings in that plastic bag and that blanket is soiled. Better fold it and put it in one of the larger bags, labelled dirty,' he said.

Dawn began to do the necessary clearing, knowing that in spite of the fact that they had finished this run, they must leave the ambulance plane ready for the next take off. A terrible thought struck her. 'You aren't going to fly it back today?'

'It depends on the weather. We were lucky to get here. Air Traffic Control wasn't very happy about it and they said that on no account may I fly until visibility has improved.'

'So, we go back on bus and ferry? I'll know my

way around this part of the world blindfolded, soon,' she said.

'We are blindfolded,' he said, 'And I for one have no intention of going as far as a ferry terminal only to be told that all ferries have been stopped. We might as well stay here and be comfortable.'

She twitched the corners of her mouth. 'I don't think Bruce was very keen on the bedroom he shared with one of the house surgeons. Do you enjoy punk-rock music until the small hours?'

'I wasn't thinking of the medical school,' he said.

'Well, let me know when we can leave, if we're flying back. I'll find out the number of the nurses' home and let you have it before you take off to wherever you are staying. It does look as if we are here for the next twelve hours at least.' She listened. 'Is that a car?'

'Yes. Get your things together and we'll drop the soiled things off at the hospital. We'll have to take the driver back before we do anything more.' She went down the steps and dragged her holdall after her. 'I'll make a last check and lock it up,' he said. 'Here . . . can you take my case?' He handed down the case, his personal luggage and the plastic bags, then turned to see that nothing was left behind. He picked up the pen that Dawn had used to make notes and stuffed it in his pocket with other odds and ends as he went out to the car. 'Everything ready in case we're called out,' he said.

They drove slowly back to the hospital and left the driver. Dawn reached in to get her case to take to the nurses' home, hoping that they could find her a room if she had to stay the night again, but Miles stopped her. 'I ought to find out where I'm sleeping,' she said.

'Leave it for a while. We need some coffee and I want to hear how our patient is getting on. Another visit might interest you. Jeff Lawson is sitting up and taking notice. We can pop in and see him.' He glanced at his watch. 'This fog is so misleading. It's quite early and we have plenty of time.' He smiled, wryly. 'The sands are running slowly now, so why not enjoy this enforced leisure.' He laughed. 'I'll ring the ward and ask if we can see him, and then I think our quest for coffee will be over. The sister there has *very* good coffee.'

'I must tidy up,' she said. 'Can I meet you here in ten minutes?' He nodded and she went to the rest room to wash and put on fresh make-up. The face that stared back from the mirror showed her that this was very necessary and she ran too much hot water, angrily, aware that she managed to look her worst when Miles Stratton was on the scene. Except in the Smugglers, she thought. I looked very good that night, even if he did look disapproving. What a mixture the man was. He could be friendly and make a girl feel as if she could depend on him in any crisis, make her believe that under the stern exterior was a man of great compassion and understanding, and yet he could shrivel her confidence with one look from those jasper-dark eyes.

She applied fresh lipstick. And he can make a girl fall in love with him even when he is being thoroughly chauvinistic, she thought. Almost defiantly, she made up her eyes to the very best advantage. It would be wasted on the nurses' home but it would give her courage to face him again when they visited Stephanie's brother . . . the brother of the woman Miles Stratton loved.

The black sweater still looked good and the auburn hair shone and curled at the ends after she had rubbed away the spots of blood from the lad's bandage that had touched her when he was struggling. She smoothed down the cord trousers and found them grubby. 'How mad I was to wear cream cords,' she thought and remembered that she had pushed an uncrushable skirt of silkly black material into her case. She tied the bright scarf that she had worn over her head when they found the boy on the cliff ledge, round her waist, linking the soft black sweater with the silky skirt, and the peacock colours glowed, showing off her tiny waist.

Miles viewed her with approval. 'You'll do,' he said.

'Why does everyone say that?'

'They don't.'

'I've had it said to me at least three times by people like Dave Attril.'

'You should feel very complimented. That's praise in these parts. I've arranged to see Jeff, but they'd like us to go there at once before he has a dressing done.' He went to the lift and held the doors back for her. 'You haven't met him, have you? Not when he was conscious?'

'No. I thought he looked like his sister,' she said, 'But I've never spoken to either of them.'

She took a deep breath as they reached the side ward where Jeff Lawson was resting, but as soon as she went into the room, she smiled. It was good to see a man looking so well, after seeing him looking like death. He greeted her warmly. 'It's wonderful to see you sitting up,' she said.

'I didn't know what I was missing.' He laughed. 'Miles told me how pretty you were, but I like to judge for myself.' She glanced at the face of the man on the other side of the bed, wondering when she had been the subject of their conversation. 'I have to thank you both for everything. Bruce told me about the new service and I had no idea I'd be the first to sample it. Bruce and Stephanie were coming over today, but they can't make it. I can't think how you flew in this fog, Miles. Must have nerves of steel.'

Coffee arrived and Dawn had the feeling that Miles was glad to have a diversion. What had he said about her to make Jeff look at her with such warmth? She accepted the cup of coffee that Miles handed to her.

'It's good that your sister can fly a plane. It takes such a long time to get here by public transport,' she said.

'That of course will come in very useful,' he said.

'I didn't know that she was joining the service. Isn't she an engineer?'

'I suppose I shouldn't say anything, but I claim the right of an invalid. I've been bursting to tell someone who knows them.' Jeff beamed. 'Perhaps you've guessed already?'

'Don't shock us too much,' said Miles with a note of genuine warning.

'A pleasant shock, I hope. Bruce and Stephanie have patched up their misunderstanding and hope to be married soon, before they go back to Australia.' He paused and looked at the frowning face of Miles Stratton. 'It was partly your fault, Miles. Bruce thought you and Stephanie had something going when she spent so much time with you planning the interior of the emergency plane.'

'There was never anything between us,' said Miles. 'Stephanie is a grand person and has been a wonderful friend and helper. She drew up plans and we had only to give them to a carpenter to have just what we wanted. I never horn in on another man's girl,' he said, firmly.

'I think it's wonderful news,' said Dawn.

'You do?' Miles stared, then poured more coffee, hiding the expression in his eyes.

'I thought that Bruce was in love with Stephanie. He tried to pretend that he wasn't interested in her, but he couldn't keep her name out of the conversation,' she said.

'I've noticed that tendency in other people, too,' said Jeff, with a wicked grin.

'Well, we ought to leave you to the tender mercies of the nurses. They want us out and we have to find somewhere to stay tonight. It's all go!' said Miles, with quite uncharacteristic heartiness.

'Ring the Manor . . . it's so near you could find it in the dark, or in a fog,' said Jeff. 'They serve good food and if you can see it tomorrow, you'll see what I mean when I say it's the prettiest pub for miles.'

'I shall be staying in the nurses' home,' said Dawn.

'Rubbish. Make a night of it. You deserve a break and I'm sure that Miles will look after you well.'

'It will be my pleasure,' he said, solemnly.

So now he's stuck with me, like it or not, she thought. 'I can stay here,' she said.

'You heard what the man said, and I agree. After being in a plane piloted by me, you deserve the best.'

'Goodbye . . . come and see me again soon,' said Jeff.

'I ought to ring the hospital and tell them we're here. Everything happened so soon that they might worry,' said Dawn when they had left Jeff's side ward.

'I've already sent a message,' said Miles, 'but I ought to ring Rock Manor. I don't want to wander round in the fog any more than we must if they can't take us.'

'I can stay here,' she said again, but he ignored her and went quickly to the pay telephone at the end of the corridor. Dawn twisted her sweater hem between nervous fingers, watching his face and listening to his side of the conversation, not knowing if she wanted to stay with him or not. She had wasted her sympathy on him over Stephanie, but there must be someone he loved, or why was he never seen in the company of any of the female staff of the St Boniface? Hadn't she heard that he wanted to make the Island his base when he joined the RAF in the autumn? A base to a man like him could only mean a real home, with a woman he loved . . . and her heart ached for that love, that home, that man.

'Everything fixed.' He grinned. 'They had several holiday cancellations due to the fog, so they offered us a four-poster bed with all the trimmings.' She gasped. 'Don't panic, I settled for two chaste single rooms.' His gaze was intent and disturbing. 'But the four-poster sounded great.'

She picked up her bag. 'Well, let's go. I'd love a really hot deep bath before we eat, this evening.' It was essential to keep to small talk and to discussion about the hotel, the food and their patient.

The hired car crawled along the driveway to an old grey house from which warm golden lights tried to beat the fog. The warmth of the log fire in the hall was sanctuary from the chill outside and the pretty bathroom attached to Dawn's room was a welcoming relief. She bathed and brushed her hair, taking her time and trying to get her mind in some sort of order. She searched through her handbag and holdall, first slowly as if she knew she could find whatever it was she sought, then more quickly, in fear. My locket! she thought. Oh, *no*! She looked round the pretty room. There was no place where she could have dropped the locket there.

A tap on the door made her start. She said an automatic 'Come in,' and went through her handbag again, tipping the contents out on the bed.

'Is this what you're looking for?' said Miles. She swung round to see him dangling her locket on its broken chain. 'Oh, thank you . . . I thought it was lost.'

'It was in the plane.' He turned it over. 'Very pretty,' he said, and made to open it.

'Don't do that,' she said.

'Why not? You once showed me the lock of hair and . . . the empty space.' He gently sat her on the edge of the bed, and opened the locket.

'No,' she said in a whisper. 'Please, Miles . . . give that to me.'

'Not until you tell me about the hair in the other side of the locket . . .' He was laughing, gently. 'You might at least have taken out the thorns first.'

She looked up, afraid, but his eyes were tender and his arms a haven from the fog, from doubt and wretchedness. He kissed her and she knew that the moment sealed her fate and her whole future. She clung to him, returning kiss for kiss until she seemed to turn to floating mist. His fingers framed her delicate, quivering cheeks. 'I thought you loved Stephanie,' she said.

'Almost as silly as my believing that there could be anything between you and Tyley,' he said. He reached across for her nail scissors in the pile of handbag contents. 'I can give you a better lock of hair than that one,' he said, but she stayed his hand.

'I'm not going to dinner with a shorn lamb,' she said. 'Besides . . . I want that one, complete with thorns, as a fitting reminder of everything that has happened between us.'

He chuckled and held her close again.

'You know . . .' he murmured later, 'that four-poster would have been a good idea.' He felt her body tense against his own. 'But later . . . we'll come back later, after the wedding. I peeped into the room, and there is a very knowing, carved cupid over one corner.'

She blushed. 'We can always draw the curtains,' she said.

Doctor Nurse Romances

Romance in the wide world of medicine

Amongst the intense emotional pressures of modern medical life, doctors and nurses often find romance. Read about their lives and loves in the other two Doctor Nurse titles available this month.

LADY IN HARLEY STREET
by Anne Vinton

It seems the answer to Dr Celia Derwent's prayers when her new boss Dr Alan Grainger proposes marriage. She desperately needs a husband in order to convince the courts that she should have custody of her orphaned niece Fiona, and Alan is devoted to Fiona. But will this marriage of convenience really solve all Celia's problems?

TROPICAL NURSE
by Margaret Barker

A six-month nursing contract in West Africa will give Kate Mathews just the time she needs to remove any doubts she has about her engagement to David, her childhood sweetheart.

Yet when her new boss, the arrogant Dr Richard Brooks echoes her doubts, why is she suddenly so determined that nothing he says will stop her marriage?

Mills & Boon
the rose of romance